The Magician's Shadow

LORI ZUPPINGER

Tea & Music

This is a work of fiction. Names, characters, businesses, places, events and incidents are either the product of the author's imagination or used in a fictitious manner. Any resemblance to actual persons, living or dead, or actual events is purely coincidental.

Cover art by Ann McDougall Design & Creative Services

To all the places on earth that still hang on to their magic
And all the people still willing to see it

ACKNOWLEDGMENTS

I'm still in a state of mild disbelief that I have books out in the wild, let alone a third one. So, my heartfelt thanks to everyone who has been kind enough to check out the first two volumes and express interest in there being a 'part three'. My gratitude also goes to all my friends & loved ones who have *very* patiently listened to my grousing about how much more difficult this book was to wrangle into something approaching a publishable state. And huge thanks and love to all those who have been kind enough to spread the word and post reviews – it's unbelievably helpful and I appreciate it more than I can possibly express.

Also, to my dad, Rick Brodhurst: I'll try to sign my name more neatly this time.

CHAPTER ONE

Flexing my fingers, I called to mind a rose.

Studying it in my memory, I began to recreate it: the deep green of the stem and its wicked thorns, the spiral nest of golden petals, tinged red round the edges. Hands moving in concert with my thoughts, I drew up the image of the bloom, not with paint or pencil, but with magic.

I hardly dared to check, but I opened my eyes and saw it hovering before me. One long-stemmed rose, a perfect exemplar of the bushes I had seen in the garden, glowing slightly as the light faded from the window and dusk entered the room. It was my best illusion yet.

In the short space between August and November, my life had been overturned more than once: finding the troupe of magicians that I had once thought only a family legend, learning I could become one of them, and running up against the reality that dangers could come along with the wonders. The fact that I had managed to advance my own skills this far along the way was a point of pride, but practice in the attic room of my friends' quiet country home was a far cry from being able to reliably call up these tricks before an audience.

I tried to picture it, to hold my focus on the rose while still imagining the quiet-yet-not of a tent with several dozen people clustered round its edges. The smell of trodden-down earth and night air and anticipation. I could almost see it all, and the rose was still there.

My breath of relief at my success was a short one. The vision of the appreciative audience turned all too real, narrowing down on one detail: a man in a red cloak and gold mask, his hand reaching for my throat. Opening my mouth, I found no sound coming out. He wrapped his fingers round my neck and began to squeeze.

I came back to myself with a gasp, and a forcible reminder that the image was not real: even less real than the rose, now long gone. Panic had never been a regular feature of my life before, but since being attacked by a rogue magician a few weeks earlier, I had been forced to learn some different sorts of tricks. *Find five things you can see, four you can touch…* Talking myself down, and grounding myself in the simple contents of the guest room – the pale blue bedspread, the scarred wooden side table with my phone and watch on top, articles of clothing draped over the back of the chair and hanging half-out of my backpack – helped me come back to reality and decide that I'd probably spent enough time alone for the moment.

Three pairs of eyes looked me over as I entered the kitchen. The senior members of the Kavanagh clan: Daniel and Molly and their son Ben. "Need a bit of a break, darling?" Ben asked. When I didn't reply, he nodded. "It's to be expected, I'm sure."

"I just keep imagining him," I replied. "It feels way too real." Since my decision to join the magicians, the Kavanagh family had all but adopted me, and recent events had led them to insist that I stay with them at their home in Ireland until the troupe met again. It was a peaceful place, and an ideal environment to practice. We certainly had not seen hide nor hair of Frederick Desrochers, the man who had threatened me in Venice and again in Germany; in fact, there had been no sign of him since some of our travelling companions had bundled him into a van bound for Romania several days earlier. But all the same, he haunted me.

Ben's father Daniel motioned to the various empty chairs around the long farmhouse table. "Have a cup of tea, and a bite of something, to settle your nerves. These things are always worst at night. You'll feel better with the sunrise."

I knew he was right, though daylight was a long way off; morning was coming later and later, as we slid closer to the end of November. County Wicklow was several degrees' latitude further north than where I had come from in southern Ontario, and the Isle of Skye, where we were headed next, was further still. Despite the prospect of stormy weather and four o'clock sunsets, though, I was impatient to get there.

CHAPTER TWO

"How much longer, do you think?" Claire asked. "We must be nearly there."

I looked out the rain-spattered window at the landscape slipping by. Mountains had subsided into hills and I was beginning to catch glimpses of the ocean. Although I had only really joined the troupe of magicians a few months before, I was already getting used to the idea that it involved a lot of overland travel, some of it less than glamorous. Claire and I were squeezed, along with our bags, into the backseat of her battered hatchback as her parents navigated the drive across Skye.

Ben turned around from the passenger seat. "Twenty minutes or so to Gavin's. Your mum and I are another five minutes down the road, at the old inn."

The island was bigger than I'd realized, and the village of Uig was almost at its extreme end. From there, we could have taken a ferry over to Harris and Lewis if we'd felt the inclination, and so when I glimpsed a black-and-white CalMac boat on the water, I knew we must be getting close. A minute or two later, a long pier came into view, off to our left on the opposite side of a bay. "That must be it."

Although I'd addressed the remark to Claire, it was her mother Colleen who answered. "That's Uig pier, but the old hostel is just up ahead, on this side of the water. It's not too far from where we'll mount the show."

Sure enough, as we came around another bend, I could see that the village was strung out in a line along the road from the pier, curving around the head of the bay towards us. The rain had lessened to more of a steady mist, the sort of thing that would have been quite pleasant on a warmer day, but it was feeling decidedly Novemberish when we pulled into a driveway in front of a rambling one-story building that looked like it had started as a typical Highland cottage and grown a few long, boxy additions. Telling us to give their regards to Gavin, Colleen and Ben dropped us off and continued on towards the village.

Claire shook her head. "I can't believe Gav bought this place. How is he going to run a hostel while we're on the road?"

"He must have some other people in on it," I replied, wondering if we should knock or just walk in. "Are we all staying here?"

"Well, anyone who doesn't mind bunking in together, I think," Claire replied. "I think they said it holds about forty or so? Mum and Dad probably aren't the only ones opting out, and I can't imagine everybody will come this late in the season, anyhow." After a quick peek in the side window, we opted to let ourselves in. "Hello?"

"Is that Claire? And Heather?" I had only seen Gavin a fortnight before, so it was a bit startling when he popped around the corner and I saw that he'd cut his hair quite a bit shorter. If it hadn't been for his faded jeans and threadbare t-shirt, he might have looked almost professional. "Come in, come in. You're almost the first, so you've got your pick of rooms."

He gave us the grand tour, describing his plans to spruce things up over the winter and have a cousin of his run the place during our travels. "You might want this one," he said, opening up the last door at the far end of the hall. "It's got probably the nicest view, and it won't be so noisy as some others."

The room, a small one with two sets of bunk beds, had a window looking out towards the bay and the hills. The carpet and paint were rather institutional and had seen better days, but as usual I could hardly find fault with free accommodation. And it would be fun, I thought, to have so many of us all staying under one roof.

"I'll leave you to it," Gavin said. "There's tea and a few snacks in the main kitchen, but I'm just off into town to get some proper food for everyone. Make yourselves at home, and if anyone else shows up, tell them to settle in and I'll be back around three."

After tossing my bag onto one of the bunks, I returned to the big open space that Gavin had called the common room. It had a motley assortment of couches and armchairs, along with a pair of dining-hall tables big enough for at least a dozen apiece. Anyone else who had already arrived must be at the carnival site, since the building was quiet as a tomb. Pulling my phone from my pocket, I sent a quick message: *We're here, in one piece.*

It was just a figure of speech, but I suspected he would be worried. Eric, my closest ally among the handful of friends I had made since joining the troupe, seemed to have designated himself as my protector as well. After I'd been threatened in Germany, he had insisted on accompanying me on my initial return to the Kavanaghs' home and it had taken a couple of days before he had been sufficiently persuaded that Frederick Desrochers was not likely to pop up in rural Ireland. Despite my nightmares, and despite how much I appreciated everyone's concern, I had a private suspicion that I would get over the experience a little quicker if everyone else stopped acting as if it was apt to recur at any moment.

Excellent. I'm getting a ride up in the van with Eleanor and the gang. Almost at Glencoe, should be there before dinner. El says save her a bottom bunk.

I smiled. There would definitely be more life in the building once Eleanor arrived. In the interim, perhaps it was time to see where the magic would actually be.

The mist was giving way to a light fog; on the other side of the bay I could still see the long ferry pier, but only just, and the damp made me glad of the wool sweater under my coat. I could have waited for Claire – could have even waited longer, for some of our group to come with a car or van – but it felt right to be walking there on my own, with nothing else to go on but Ben's vague mention that it was 'down the Balnaknock road'. It felt right to discover it on my own.

I found the sideroad easily enough, just a stone's throw from the hostel. For a little while, it led up a hill, almost paralleling the main road, but at the crest it turned inland, near a small cemetery. Past that, there were fields – sloping down to my left and up to my right – and the occasional stand of evergreen trees. With the fog, I couldn't tell much of what might lay in the distance. Passing three houses reasonably close together, I thought I might be coming into a small hamlet, but the fields continued on. Nothing but the occasional bleating of sheep could be heard.

Despite the otherworldly feel of the place and the weather, I had only been walking twenty minutes or so when I heard voices; they seemed simultaneously close at hand and far away. At last, rounding a bend in the road, I saw shapes I recognized through the mist: a van pulled off into an open field and a cluster of silhouettes showing up dark against a large, pale tent. The shortest figure stepped away from the group and met me halfway between the tent and the road.

"Heather? I was wondering who was coming along the road there."

"Hi, Arthur." I had only met Arthur Bradburn a few times, but his son had become a good friend, despite being half my age. "Is Luke with you?"

Arthur laughed and shook his head. "He took a lift into town with Gavin. A bit boring for him, standing about with all these old men."

I looked at the one tent, and the small group of people. "Are we starting tonight? I thought a lot of people weren't coming in till tomorrow."

He chuckled, looking almost sheepish. "Ah, well. We took advantage of the fog to get a little practice in. Try something new, you see? Well, you'll see tomorrow," he added, with a broad wink. "But you'll want to see the glen, of course. It's just there."

Where he had pointed, all I could make out was a tiny ridge of hills that seemed not much bigger than a row of houses. "The glen?"

"The Fairy Glen, of course. I'm surprised the Kavanaghs didn't tell you more about it."

I wondered why I hadn't thought to ask them. This whole business of travelling round doing magic in strange locations was quite a learning curve. "What's there?"

Arthur shooed me in that general direction. "Just go and have a look."

His direction had been vague, but I set off that way, assuming I would know it when I saw it. If nothing else, I knew I would come back to the road I had walked in on, so there was no real fear of getting lost. As I came closer to the ridge, I noticed that the slopes had a curiously wrinkled appearance, as if the turf had been taken out of the laundry wet and draped carelessly over the features beneath.

Climbing up and over, I found myself walking down into one of the strangest landscapes I'd ever seen in real life. It looked like it should have been a set for a children's fantasy show, all miniature conical hills and wizened, four-foot-high witch hazel trees. I crossed the road, passing a tiny pond, and found myself looking up at an outcropping of rocks that vaguely resembled a castle, if a fairly diminutive one. It was the highest feature visible through the fog, and it drew my eye. There, I suspected, was the centre of the energy that I could already vaguely feel in the air about this place.

I circled around the west end of it – though my conscious mind wanted to think it was north, my unorthodox magical training had given me a pretty good inner compass if I paid attention – and came to another little valley, smoother and greener than I might have expected. Someone had laid out stones in a small circular labyrinth, and though the formation didn't seem to have any particular energy of its own I took the time to walk it, letting my feet slowly trace out the path as I tried to get the sense of what the Fairy Glen was. The places I had been with the magicians had all had power, necessary to us to fuel our gifts, but each one had had a distinct flavor: the electric current of Callanish, the vaguely unsettling hum of the megaliths at Wéris in Belgium, and the comforting solidity of the pagan wall in Bad Dürkheim. I couldn't quite put my finger on what the Fairy Glen felt like to me, not yet, but I felt welcome, and that was a start.

CHAPTER THREE

Perhaps because I was not used to how short the days were becoming, or perhaps because the fog had made things so dim to begin with, twilight caught me by surprise as I was still exploring the glen. Although it was only ten to four by my watch, the vague pale ghost of the sun was no longer visible in the west. In the coming nights I would be out much later, but I wasn't in a rush to test whether I could find my way back to the hostel alone in full darkness and fog.

The wind was picking up a little, and I noticed belatedly that the mist had stopped; as I passed the trio of houses halfway along the road I could see that the fog was blowing away inland. By the time I regained the main road, the air was clear – though noticeably colder with the breeze off the ocean – and there were even a few patches of sky opening up in the west, revealing a last purple hint of sunset behind the clouds. Across the water, the pier was illuminated, and the scattered lights of the village made an elegant curve round the head of the bay. There were no streetlights on my side, though, and the late afternoon was well on its way to what my city-dwelling brain categorized as 'country dark'.

Coming up the drive to the hostel, I could see that our numbers had grown. Two white vans were parked out front, along with a couple of cars, and many of the building's windows were lit. Conscious that I was damp and muddy, I wondered if the back door by the dormitories might be open, but the front door opened before I could decide. I saw Eleanor's outline in the doorway for a second before she made her way out to the van.

"Christ, Heather," she said, startling visibly as I walked up out of the darkness. "I didn't see you there. You might want to let them know you're back; when we heard you'd wandered off a couple of hours ago he was about to go looking for you."

"I wish he'd stop being so paranoid, honestly." There was no need to ask who she was talking about: Eric, of course. "It makes me feel like a time bomb."

She shrugged, before opening the back of the van. "With his dad dying, and everything, I think appointing himself as your bodyguard probably feels like something he can actually control. But…" Rummaging among the backpacks and bags, she trailed off.

"What?"

"I get the impression it's a bit of an excuse, too." Pulling out a shoulder bag, she looked up at me, her nose crinkling on one side. "It's got to still be a bit raw. I lost my mum when I was nineteen."

"I'm sorry."

She nodded. "And there was this weird time in between where I was trying to get back to normal but not quite making it yet. I think he's there, and he's more comfortable with you than with some."

Hearing it put like that, I repented my minor impatience. "Good point. I'll go in before he starts a search party."

I came through the empty vestibule into a crowd in the common room; magicians were slouched on sofas, gathered round the long tables, meandering in and out from the hallway that led to the dorms. After a look around and greetings to some familiar faces – only some of whom seemed to notice me – I continued into the kitchen.

Eric was leaning on the counter, unopened beer in hand, watching Gavin unload groceries from the numerous bags on the counters and the floor.

"Good," I announced. "I haven't missed dinner, then."

I could see Eric's posture relax. "In fact, you're just in time to get drafted into making it. You want to give us a hand?"

There had to be at least thirty people out there, if not more, but the kitchen was clearly made for that sort of thing, with multiple stoves and a lot of workspace. I shrugged. "Hey, I'd certainly rather cook than clean. What are we making?"

Gavin rummaged through the bags. "Sausages… pasta… lentils and rice, I'll do those… and some salad."

As he produced two entire bags of various green leafy things, I did a double-take. "And here I thought I might not see salad till I went back to Canada. Are you sure you're Scottish, Gavin?"

"He has lived in England for quite a while," Eric pointed out, in what sounded like a reasonable tone. "Although I don't know how much of a difference that makes. He's worked in kitchens," he added, after Gavin made a rude gesture and went back to unpacking groceries. "Used to work as a short-order cook in the off season, sometimes."

"Saved you from being a literal starving artist," Gavin replied.

As I set about chopping vegetables for a pasta sauce, I listened to them bantering back and forth. Though Eric and I had become close friends in a relatively short time, there was still a great deal I didn't know about him; little bits of their conversation, things that were old hat between them, were filling in pieces of the puzzle.

The three of us made a good team, and within about an hour we had enough food prepared to suit an army, even without using magic to extend the meal. Gavin took a plate with some of everything, and joined the crowd at one of the long tables.

"So Gavin was the one you lived with in that squat, in London?" I asked, leaning against the counter. Eric had told me a little about sharing an abandoned Brixton house with magicians and artists in his early days with the troupe, but hadn't named names.

He nodded. "Gav and another guy, Mick. I don't think you've met him; he only comes around a couple of times a year these days. Hard to believe it was twenty-five years ago. Do you want to just eat in here?" He gestured out at the common room.

I could see that there were still seats available at the big tables, but the relative quiet of the kitchen suited me. We chatted a bit more about his early days in London, and with the troupe, until it seemed that the others were mostly done traipsing in and out of the room. "How are you doing?" I was tempted to ask if he was sleeping any better, but the dark circles under his eyes gave me a clue.

"Better. I'm getting there, anyhow," he said. "I worked on some painting this week, for the first time since… Well, it helped. You?"

I waited a moment, so as not to speak through a mouthful of food. "The same, I think. Minus the painting, obviously. I've had a few more of the nightmares and flashbacks, but less so this past week. I think it'll be better here."

He smiled. "Me too."

CHAPTER FOUR

I found myself wide awake before eight the next morning. A peek out the window showed a sky just starting to brighten; despite the hour it was just barely dawn. An idea hit me. Grabbing the first halfway clean change of clothes I came across, I hastily dressed, brushed my teeth, and took off out the door. I might have to jog part of the way – I hadn't really paid close attention to how quickly the sun rose – but since I was up before sunrise, I wanted to see it from the glen.

The sky was streaked with thin wisps of cloud, showing as smudges of lilac-grey against a canvas of blues and pinks. It was chilly, but the damp in the air wasn't as penetrating as it had been the day before. A few birds were awake, and sheep somewhere; a dog barked once or twice off in the distance. I might have been the only human in the world, though.

Where I had seen the one tent, the field was empty. I knew it would be full in a few hours' time. One more bend in the road, and the Fairy Glen was before me, the tiny pond as still as a mirror, scarcely a leaf moving on the gnarled witch hazel trees as I passed.

The rock outcropping was stark against the brightening sky. It hadn't occurred to me the day before to wonder whether there was a way to climb it, but it seemed as if there was a path of sorts. Wondering whether it had been made by humans or sheep, I picked my way up it, glancing over my shoulder now and then to check the progress of the dawn. The ridge below the outcrop was sharp, and though it was not tremendously high I had to take a moment to feel confident in my balance. But the path did continue up. It was more than a little precarious – I didn't really want to think about coming back down – and there was an awkward squeeze through some rocks at the end, but I eventually popped out onto the nearly-flat top of the rock.

The sky had taken on a paler hue, the undersides of the clouds glowing a warm gold as the sun crept closer, finally edging over the horizon. It would be a short day, but it looked like it would be a fine one, and the sunlight had the orange tinge of late fall as the first rays struck me on my high perch while the ground below was still bathed in shadow. Although the grass was wet, I managed to find a rocky spot to sit down. As I did so, I could have sworn I heard someone speaking. Turning my head in every direction, I saw nothing; the glen was empty and still. Perhaps a door had briefly opened in a house out of sight, or a car had passed – but I didn't think so. It wasn't my first time hearing voices. I hoped it was something to do with the place, and not another unpleasant reaction to my experience in Germany.

To steer myself away from that particular train of thought, I decided to practice. Nothing too flashy – not that I was yet capable of much magic that could be described as 'flashy' – but I started with the rose I had practiced at the Kavanaghs'. Once it was visible before me, I experimented with changing its colour and making it move around me. Next, I had the idea to try transforming its shape into something else, but after several less-than-successful attempts I decided it was enough for one morning.

The sun was well up, illuminating nearly all of the glen, by the time I climbed down from the rocky height. Still thinking about how I could shift the rose into something else, I didn't notice I was no longer alone until I heard my name. I nearly tumbled off the ridge before I realized that Ben was in the middle of the glen, on the side away from the road.

"You gave me a fright," I said, picking my way down. "When did you get here?"

"Just now. I had an inkling I might find you here; I know how you like to wander off." Before I could take umbrage at this, he carried on. "There's something we need to talk about."

I fell into step with him, wondering if we were going anywhere in particular. "What is it? It's not –"

"Not Desrochers, no," he replied, having guessed my first thought. While I took a relieved breath, he pressed on. "But I've talked to the elders, and some of them are concerned about having you in a visible position right now. Performing, that is."

I wasn't sure what to do with this information. "Some… not all, I take it?"

He shrugged. "For my part, I'm not worried. You handled yourself just fine in Germany, Desrochers was last seen headed for Romania in an addled state, and Eleanor was onto him before he caused any serious trouble. There's those that agree with me, and those that don't."

And some who had their own issues with me. "Isabella was one of the latter, I assume." It wasn't a question. A matriarch in her own right, she resented me for being a distant relation, and for having received the blessing of her father – my great-grandfather – on his deathbed.

Ben ignored the observation. "They took it to Sofia in the end, and she said she would speak with you herself. But she agreed that you shouldn't be performing, this time."

"What?" Granted, I was hardly a star magician. I had been a supporting player, at best, to Luke in Belgium and to Eric in

Germany. And although I'd been working to improve upon my limited skills, I hadn't had any particular plans for our sojourn in Skye. But I didn't know what this meant. "Sofia said herself that I was part of the group. Is she changing her mind?"

"No, no." He held up his hands, palms out. "Don't get ahead of yourself. Nobody's sending you away, and you're not being marched to the headmaster's office here. You've done nothing wrong."

"So what do I do?" Realizing that my tone sounded petulant, I took a breath and considered. "What should I do now?"

"Talk to Sofia. I'll take you there now, if you like."

We strode along in silence, back out to the main road; there we turned downhill towards the village proper. Like so many other places I'd been in Scotland, Uig was a string of tidy whitewashed houses, mostly one-and-a-half storey, strung in a line along the road. Just past a small church, Ben stopped in front of a house much like the others. Nothing about the place suggested that it was playing host to an ancient woman who was known as an oracle to a company of travelling magicians. White lace curtains hung in the two front windows, and the little garden still bore a few flowers, bravely holding out against the chilly temperature and diminishing daylight. The faded yellow of a stand of yarrow gave me a sudden sense of disconnection; the exact same variety grew along my own front walk, back in Toronto. How much longer would I stay connected to that place?

"Alright, darling?"

Ben's voice shook me out of my momentary distraction. "Yes, fine. I was just… It doesn't matter."

"Don't worry. You're one of us now, no matter what happens. Come on."

His knock was answered by a grandmotherly lady, who ushered me in and showed me to the sort of living room that looked like it was rarely used. After a minute or two, Sofia came in. This was our third meeting, and I wondered yet again how old she might really be. Her standing among the magicians certainly suggested that she must be among the eldest of the elders. Raffaele, my long-lost great-grandfather, had lived to one hundred thirty-eight among this company. He had been frail at the end, and Sofia, though delicate, was not. Even so, it would no longer surprise me if I were to learn that she was even older than he had been.

"It is a strange thing, to begin this life," she said, after taking a seat in the floral armchair across from me. "It was ever so. And yet, you have had a stranger beginning than some."

Compared to our previous encounters, this was practically a monologue. "And what would you suggest I do?" I asked, choosing my tone carefully. I wasn't sure how I liked the idea of a council of elders – most of them unknown to me – deciding my fate, but then again, it had been my decision to join their community.

As she had done each time we had met, Sofia took my hands and examined them, occasionally murmuring something that might have been magic words, or perhaps just her mother tongue. Then she surprised me by moving her hands up to cradle my face, holding me still while she stared intently into my eyes. It was a most unnerving experience.

"There are shadows over you," she finally pronounced. "Something yet to be resolved."

"Desrochers?" I didn't like referring to him by his first name; it made him too human.

The old woman shook her head. "The memory hangs heavy on you; this much I see. It unsettles you, and others. But he is not what stops you from performing."

As much as I was trying to be respectful and polite, I couldn't quite maintain my reserve. "I thought it was you, stopping me performing."

She shook her head. "I advise. Most have found that they profit by heeding that advice. Take the stage now, if you truly feel you must, but it will not dispel the shadow."

"And what is this… shadow, then?"

"I cannot say." I wondered if she truly could not, or would not. "You will need to discover for yourself. But while you are in shadow, you cannot know your path. And until you can do that, you will not fully grasp your magic."

I sat back in the chair, pondering this. Everything had happened so quickly: from my first actual encounter with the magicians to this moment had been less than four months. Surely no one could be expected to 'fully grasp' the realities of magic in that short a time.

"Your path has been a short one, and eventful," Sofia said, echoing my thoughts. "Raffaele thrust you into our midst like a comet, when he unlocked your birthright with his dual blessing. Many of us were too swayed by his death to give you guidance, nor a true apprenticeship. You have not been given the time to dispel the shadows from others' vision of you, much less your own." Folding her hands together, she leaned forward, suddenly looking less like a mystic. "Whatever is hanging over you is not your fault, and only you can say how long you will need to vanquish it. But look into the corners of your mind, to the thoughts you do not allow yourself to take hold of. That is where the shadows lie."

By the time I left my meeting with the oracle, it was a little after ten-thirty, my phone held more than one text inquiring as to my whereabouts, and my stomach was reminding me that I had gone off without breakfast. But I needed to think over Sofia's words before I rejoined the crowd at the hostel. If nothing else, I needed to determine what I would be doing when evening fell. The post office held a small shop; I bought a snack to tide me over, replied to the texts saying I'd be back in an hour or so, and set off along the road in the opposite direction to the hostel and the glen. I had no specific destination in mind, only a need to keep my feet mindlessly moving forward in order to free my brain to ponder. The memory of a voice came back to me: *Which way will you choose?*

It was true that I'd had no proper apprenticeship or formal introduction to the life of a magician – not that Eric and the Kavanaghs hadn't worked hard to fill the gaps – and I had jumped into performing in less time than it took some newcomers to even decide to join the group. It had all been a bit of a blur, from meeting them to joining them, processing Eric's disappearance and return and all the drama that had followed. Maybe it was a good thing to take stock, after all. But my own shadows? The thoughts in the corners of my mind that I didn't allow myself to think about? I wasn't sure an hour's walk around Uig was going to be enough to work those out.

To my mind, the obvious thing hanging over me was the aftermath of my run-ins with Desrochers: the nerves and nightmares he had left in his wake. I wasn't sure the experience would ever completely leave me, but with the help of my friends I had already made great strides in getting past it. *But he is not what stops you from performing*, she had said. I tried to attack the question with logic, running through anything else I could think of as I trudged along the bay to the pier and turned back again.

It was as I came back towards the little house near the church that it struck me, jarred back into my brain by that familiar patch of yarrow, and its echo of my home in Canada. I still *had* a home in Canada, still stuffed with all my familiar belongings and awaiting my return. There was a flight booked in my name, heading back there in a few short weeks. I could walk away. Treat it all as a grand adventure, some kind of extended vacation, and pick up the threads of my established life almost as if nothing had happened.

Half a minute's thought was all it took to reject the notion as profoundly unappealing, but that door was still very much open to me. It would be so easy. Could that be the shadow that Sofia had danced around in our conversation? Had I not made it clear enough – to the magicians, to the universe, maybe to myself – that I wanted this to be my life?

By the time I climbed back up the hill to the hostel, I had the beginning of a plan.

CHAPTER FIVE

"Is Gavin around?" I glanced around the common room, not seeing him anywhere.

Eric was there, though, and he looked surprised at the question. "Probably in his room. Why?"

"I need to use his computer; I assume he's got one. There's some things I need to get organized, and it's too hard to do it on my phone. Stuff back home." When it became clear that he was getting up to follow me, I belatedly noticed the look on his face. "Not immediately or anything. But before I go home for the holidays, I need to sort some things out."

We found Gavin in the older part of the building, the original cottage. "Of course; computer's through there," he replied, when I asked my question. "I'll leave you to it."

With Eric still following me, I stepped through the door Gavin had pointed at and found myself in the bedroom. It was clearly still very much a work in progress, full of half-emptied boxes, but there was a laptop, plugged in and sitting open on the only piece of furniture in the room, the bed. "I swear I can manage this on my own," I said, raising my eyebrows. "And if you hang out in here with me, people really will talk. I'll give you a full rundown on everything, once I get done with this. What time do we need to go and set up the tents?"

Eric glanced out the window. "Couple of hours?"

"I won't need that long. Give me half an hour to set some things in motion."

"I'll hold you to that. Meet me at the pub down the road and we can talk."

My flight home was already booked: Glasgow to Toronto on the fifteenth of December. When I would be coming back, and where to, would have to remain a question mark, though I couldn't help spending a few minutes looking through listings of properties for sale in various parts of the UK, as well as back home. Immigration information I had already looked up, but I checked through it again just to be sure. Then there were the emails to compose. I tackled the most challenging one first:

Hi Dad,

First off, you'll be glad to hear that I am in fact coming back for Christmas. You may be less thrilled, although maybe not surprised, to hear that I'm not staying.

Please don't say anything to Mum yet. I want to talk to her face to face, but the reason I'm mentioning it now is that I need your help with some paperwork. I think you said that you looked up your father's birth certificate once – do you still have it? If not, I can get a copy over here before I fly home, but if by any chance you know his birthdate it would help a lot, since it's a pretty common name.

I also need your long-form birth certificate (not the regular kind that you keep in your wallet, it has to be one showing your parents' names); I can't request that myself, but if you could order that now (I'll pay you back the fee, obviously), then I can get the paperwork going when I'm home, so that I can legally stay in the UK.

I can tell you more about it when I see you in a few weeks.

Love, Heather

By the time I had finished and made it down the hill to the pub, Eric had already ordered me a drink and was impatient for details on what I had been up to. Leaping past the conversation with Sofia — certainly the salient point of the morning as far as I was concerned — he seized on other logistics. "So you're selling your house?"

I nodded, taking a small sip of cider. "I feel a bit bad, since I'd told my cousin she could rent it till April, but she didn't seem too bothered — said she would probably share a place with some friends, closer to campus."

"Will it sell that fast?"

"In Toronto, these days? I think so. That's really the least of my worries, to be honest." I shrugged. "At least, I'm hoping that's the case, because I don't want to have to spend months there dealing with it before I can come back."

Eric nodded. "Well, if it's any consolation, we can always meet up halfway. Niagara Falls?"

"You're going back for Christmas?"

"I feel like I need to, this year." With a sigh, he shifted his pint glass on the table but did not take a drink. "First one without my dad, and all. But you won't miss too much here over the winter; it's pretty quiet in December and January, although some of us usually do something somewhere, unofficially, for New Year's. I'll obviously have to take a pass on that this year. If you get back by February, there'll be something in the south, maybe south of France or Spain or somewhere it's a bit warmer. But if you have to miss it, it's okay." We sat in comfortable silence for a while, before he asked his next question. "Any thought on where you'll stay when you come back?"

We were still brainstorming on that particular topic as we walked towards the Fairy Glen, a few rays of weak November sunshine breaking through the low cloud. I knew I would continue to find a welcome in Ireland with the Kavanaghs for as long as I liked, but I wanted to have my own space, even if it was only to come back to here and there between travels.

"The thing is," I said, as we turned down the Balnaknock road. "I'll need some kind of... a day job, I guess, for lack of a better word. But I can't think of a damn thing that would work around all this."

Eric tilted his head. "Maybe, maybe not. Some people here just do this, and maybe pick up a bit of busking in between."

"Yeah, but most of them have families who bought property a hundred years ago. The Kavanaghs rent out their grazing lands. I'm sure others have some kind of other thing like that, that more or less runs itself."

"Apparently you've owned property for twenty years," he countered.

I did the math in my head. "Fifteen. I was lucky; my granny left me some money back when houses were cheap."

"So? If you get enough from selling your place to buy a flat or something here, then you just need enough money to cover pretty basic bills – light, heat, phone, council tax – and some transportation when we go from place to place."

"True." I'd had much the same thought. But it all seemed to go around in circles in my head: too many question marks and possibilities.

As if guessing my train of thought, Eric stopped on the road and turned to face me. "If money, and work, and all of it, wasn't an issue, where would you want to be?"

I took a breath and looked around. "Part of me is awfully tempted by the idea of an old stone house on Lewis, somewhere like Callanish. Or maybe Leurbost, where my family came from. Or around here. But I think the isolation might get to me a bit – living alone in a rural place is *really* living alone, you know?" I paused, thinking he was about to say something, but he gestured for me to carry on. "And it wouldn't be that practical for joining up with everybody. Or anything, really. I don't want to have to deal with getting my driver's license here and having a car."

"True. I haven't owned a car since I left the States. I did eventually get my British license, though."

"And on the other hand, there's so many great cities. London's out of my league, but I've always kind of had an idle dream of living in Edinburgh, probably since the first time I came to Scotland. What?" This time, there was definitely something he wasn't saying.

"I…" He drew the syllable out. "It's just funny you should say that, because I might be moving up there myself sometime soon. There's nothing particularly inspiring about where I am right now, other than that it's convenient to the Continent. I told you about Mick, my other artist friend?"

"You said he doesn't join the show that often anymore."

"The art drew him in more," he explained. "A while back, he partnered up with some other folks – not magicians – and started an artist-run centre in Leith. He's been bugging me to join them ever since. I'd never give this up," he added immediately, "but they don't need me to actively run the place, just curate some shows, plan their calendar, maybe give a workshop or two in the off-season. I've been seriously thinking about taking them up on it for about a year now, but just haven't gotten around to really acting on it yet. But once I get the holidays out of the way, and things settled back home, I'm pretty sure I'm going to. I don't know if that'll bias you for or against living there yourself, though," he added, laughing.

"Well, one thing at a time," I replied, unable to help laughing along. Coming around the bend in the road, I could see the tents rising. "Don't tell anyone else about this just yet, okay? I've got too much to still figure out."

"Your secret's safe with me. In the meantime, what are you actually going to do tonight? Are you really not performing?"

I shook my head. "I'm not sure what I think about Sofia and this 'shadow', but I do think it's fair that I should pay some dues around here. I'll find something to help out with."

CHAPTER SIX

Helping Eric set up his tent, I did have some second thoughts, remembering how it felt to stand in front of an audience. I watched him practice for a few minutes, marveling once again at how effortlessly it all came to him. Not just the fact that his magical skills were years beyond mine, but the way that the ideas seemed to materialize out of thin air, like the mists themselves. A panther faded, and I found Eric looking at me. It was all I could do not to get off the bench and join in.

"Are you sure?" he asked again.

Standing up, I nodded. "Absolutely." I would have to leave him to it, or become a distraction. Besides, I still needed to find myself a way to be useful. Working with Eleanor seemed the obvious choice, but – precisely because that would be the easiest way out – I cast about for another idea.

Circling round the aisles of tents, I was so busy thinking of ways to pitch in that I didn't have much attention for the people around me. But when I glanced up and saw Isabella heading my way, I froze, a mixture of nerves and anger welling up. I didn't need anyone's confirmation to know that she would have been one of the voices speaking against me to the elders – and I certainly didn't need another run-in with her. *Just go away*, I thought.

To my relieved surprise, she made a sharp turn and headed into a nearby tent before reaching me. Not wanting to wait around to bump into her again, I ducked down another alley and popped out by the entrance to the field. The ticket booth was empty, but I sat down there until someone came along. I had seen the woman before; in fact, her spectacular silver braids were part of the indelible memory of my first time buying a ticket myself.

"Mari...anne?" I ventured, knowing it was not quite right.

"Marisol. You look like you're making yourself comfortable here." Her tone was a mixture of amusement and exasperation.

"I thought I could... help out."

She laughed. "Everyone new always thinks they should start out by selling the tickets, as if this is how to prove they can be trusted with more elevated things."

My mouth hung open for a moment. "I'm sorry... I didn't mean it like that..."

"It's alright. I didn't take it like that."

There wasn't too much to learn – which was a good thing, since the sun was already starting to disappear behind the hills. Once dusk descended, it was only a matter of time before headlights started coming up the road, moving slowly to avoid silhouetted figures walking along the verge. I had thought that the first arrivals might be the young people, but I should have known better than to make assumptions. Two couples, maybe in their early sixties, were my first customers, and all four of them wore expressions of excitement that took years off their faces.

"We kept wondering when you'd be back," one of the women said, as her husband handed over a fifty-pound note for the four of them. "It's been what… six years now?"

"Seven," her husband corrected her. "It was in two thousand and six. Remember we were just back from Inverness, from Katie's wedding?"

"Oh, right you are. I don't remember you, though, my dear," she said, turning her gaze back to me as I passed them their change and drew the glowing symbol on her hand. She didn't have to know that the marker was just a prop, that there was no ink in that sigil on her skin. "You must be new since then?"

"Quite new," I agreed. Although I declined to elaborate, I could see their attention sharpen, and after they walked away I was quite sure I heard *'American!'* in a startled undertone. I supposed I would have to get used to that.

As it was the first evening – and a Monday evening, to boot – I wasn't surprised that attendance was on the modest side. Most of the other visitors were less chatty on arrival, but all bore a look of anticipation that warmed my heart: to be a part of something that brought this kind of joy to people was something I could feel good about, even if at the moment I was doing nothing that they would remember.

After a while, it seemed that anyone who was liable to come was probably already inside; it had been fifteen minutes or more since anyone had approached the booth. Night had fallen so long ago that I was sure it must be well on towards midnight, but a glance at my watch proved that it was only a few minutes to ten when two people wandered over from inside the carnival.

"I could sit for a while." Marisol set down a plate of food and came around the counter, motioning for me to get up. "You needn't miss the whole evening."

"Are you sure?"

She waved me away. "Go on, while the Feast is still there. I'm quite fine."

Eleanor had come along with her, and she leaned forward, both elbows on the counter, chin resting on her hands. "Come on. I'm doing my rounds and catching a couple of performances. And there's something I wanted to talk to you about."

I asked immediately, of course, but she just shook her head. "Let's walk a bit. I'll explain somewhere quieter. It's not a crisis," she added, waving a hand. "Just something I wanted to check on. But Marisol's right, let's go grab something to eat before they take the Feast down."

The golden-orange tent stood square in the middle of the main thoroughfare of the carnival, a queue of people still snaking out the entrance and a variety of enticing smells wafting our way. We cut in through the magicians' entrance and surveyed the heavily-laden tables, the food and drink suited to a long chilly November night. Helping myself to a toasted cheese sandwich and a mug of hot cider, I slipped out again, though not without making a mental note to come back for bread pudding if the tent was still up later.

Eleanor followed, with a steaming cup of what smelled like tomato soup. "Let's sit and watch something. I don't trust myself to walk around with this."

The nearest lit tent was striped in indigo and black and would have nearly disappeared into the night if it had not had lighter colours nearby. I didn't remember having seen it before, but that didn't mean much; some mainstays of the show used the same tent every time, but many people varied their performance and setup each stop or even each night. We had missed the beginning, and the tent was crowded, but once we found a vantage point I couldn't help an exclamation.

"Holy shit," I added, much more quietly, near Eleanor's ear. "I was wondering what Gavin did."

It was indeed Gavin, along with two other magicians – a man and a woman, both of whom I had seen in passing but could not put names to – and what they were doing was levitating about eighteen inches above the grassy floor in the centre of the circle. I was tempted to remain standing so as to have a better view of what they were up to, but Eleanor had already found space on a back bench and was gesturing for me to sit. We did not speak – not while the performance was going on – and as I watched, I reflected yet again on how little I still knew about what went on in this strange community. Gavin had brought an attractive woman up from the first row of benches and was supporting her with one hand as she floated up overhead, her eyes wide as dinner plates. Was he flirting with her? He wasn't married, I knew that much, but was he involved with anyone – perhaps the auburn-haired woman performing with him? I didn't have a vested interest, of course, not in that sense, but I found myself curious about him.

I supposed I was curious about Eric, really. Gavin was one of his first and oldest friends among this company; I wondered what their lives had been like as younger men, spending their off months in squalid rooms in Brixton, dabbling in art. I wondered what Eric's friends thought of how much time he had been spending with me.

As the performance came to a close, I gave myself a shake. It was probably fortunate that Eleanor couldn't read minds – or at least, I assumed that I would have heard about it if she did – because she would certainly interpret my train of thought the wrong way.

"So what next?" I added, once we were almost the last ones left on the benches.

Eleanor pointed out that we should take our mugs back to the food tent, and I wondered if she was deliberately stalling on whatever it was she wanted to talk about. However, I had never seen where they actually prepared the Feast, so the long, low tent camouflaged behind a small grassy berm was a diversion. I was surprised to see Claire there, flour smeared on her cheek, up to her elbows in soap suds as she took the two silver mugs from us and added them to the bin of washing-up.

"Are you not performing?" I asked, wondering if I should grab a dish towel and pitch in.

"I've already done," she replied, not really looking up as she continued with her task. "I went on early. I was thinking to do another one later, but I'm feeling a bit worn out. Sometimes it takes a day to get back in the swing of things."

"Maybe just call it a night, then. Get some rest," Eleanor suggested, before she motioned me out of the way of an older man using magic to stack plates into a wooden crate. "Showoff," she said under her breath as we exited the tent. "Some things are honestly easier the normal way. Anyhow. I wanted to ask you – did you have a run-in with Isabella earlier?"

I knew Eleanor used magic to track the comings and goings of the show, but I hadn't realized just how much detail she paid attention to. "No. I thought I was about to; she was headed right for me but turned and went somewhere else at the last second."

"Okay. I saw you head different directions so quickly that I wondered if something had been said. Maybe she's finally letting it go."

I thought about the fact that I was banned from performing, but said nothing, just waved Eleanor off when she had to get back to the security tent. Left to my own devices again, I was considering heading back to the ticket booth when I saw Claire hurrying past me, seemingly headed for the glen and still looking

very much out of sorts. I would have minded my own business —
after all, heading to a source of magic to recharge was sometimes
just as good as a physical rest — if I hadn't noticed a man in the
shadows, following her as she left the boundaries of the field. I
trailed him.

Claire was well ahead of me, just a silhouette in the moonlight,
but something must have spooked her; she startled and ran, not
into the glen but away down the road toward the hostel. The man's
figure hesitated, but did not pursue her. Debating my options, I
decided that I didn't want to face him down on my own. Trusting
that Eleanor would have noticed something, and keeping an ear
out for any footsteps coming after me, I headed towards the hostel
as well. It seemed as if there were entirely too many magicians
being followed around lately, but two didn't make a trend. I hoped.

CHAPTER SEVEN

There was no chance to talk to Claire that night, but I found her in a quiet moment after breakfast, when at least half of our compatriots were still asleep. I decided to keep it simple.

"It looked like someone was following you to the glen last night."

A strange look crossed her face. "I might have known someone would see that."

"Are you alright?"

She took a deep breath and turned her back to me, looking out the window. "It's beautiful out. Can we talk outside?"

It was, in fact, damp and perhaps six degrees at best, but by late-November standards she was right; the sun was flitting in and out behind clouds as the last of the morning's rain blew off towards the mainland. I didn't have my heavy coat with me, but not wanting to give her a chance to change her mind about talking, I just zipped up my fleece and hoped for the best.

"Do you remember I told you that I almost got married once?"

Surprised at the apparent non-sequitur, I nodded. "Wait, was that him last night?"

She looked out towards the sea, fiddling with the end of her braid. "I was just about finished my act – I never really pay attention to who's in the seats till I'm about at the end – and I looked at them all and thought I saw Brendan standing there. I panicked and just left. I don't even remember if I took a bow, just ran off to catch my breath. Doing the washing-up is usually a good way to settle my nerves. I'd just about convinced myself that I'd been seeing things, and went off to the glen to get my head back on straight, but when I realized someone was coming after me I knew it must be him."

"Are you sure you're okay?" I asked, frowning.

"It's not like that." Claire shook her head. "I'm not afraid of him. It's not... I just... Brendan is a lovely man. If he was a magician – or if I was a normal girl – I'd have married him in a heartbeat. But I couldn't. And I couldn't tell him why. It didn't end well."

I thought about this for a moment. "If he saw you perform..."

"Even if he did, how could I explain?"

The question stuck in my mind through the evening, as I helped out behind the scenes. Partly out of curiosity about this Brendan, I had taken Eleanor up on her suggestion that I assist in the security tent, although I kept Claire's confidence about the matter.

Magicians sometimes did wind up with non-magical partners, I was sure. Ben had been prepared to marry Eric's mother once, and from all I had heard of the matter, one of the options had been for her to join them. My own Granny Chrissie had at least entertained the idea that she might run off with Raffaele, though as it happened he never asked her to. How did it all work? Were there husbands and wives at home somewhere, explaining the frequent absences of their magician spouse as 'travelling on business'? I was beginning to think that the spots where magic intersected directly with everyday life were stranger and more confusing than the existence of magic in the first place.

Around eleven, I decided to take a break and watch Claire perform. I wanted to take her at her word and believe that Brendan was harmless, but after my own experience of having someone seek me out at a performance, part of me wanted to keep an eye on her.

I made my way towards her tent, shivering a little in the night air. The cold certainly had not deterred the visitors, more numerous than the night before. Most of them were walking from tent to tent with purpose rather than lingering outdoors for too long, but a crowd gathered at the end of the main aisle caught my attention. Taking a detour in that direction, I found something like a fountain: a broad, shallow pool set in what seemed to be dark stone, about waist height and with tall jets in the centre that might have been phoenixes. However, rather than gushing water, the figures were spouting fire; it arced from their beaks in a stream and flickered across the surface of the pool. Even several paces away I could feel the warmth against my face.

The unexpected sight nearly distracted me from my errand, and I stood for a while, entranced by it, until a hand on my back shocked me out of my reverie.

"Sorry, I didn't mean to scare you," Eric said. "Nice, isn't it?"

I nodded, then turned to look at him more closely. Something about his tone was different. It took me a moment for my brain to register: he looked happier than I had seen since before his father had passed. In fact, I might have almost ventured to call it glee. Before I could ask, he spoke again. "Guess who did it."

Looking from Eric to the fire fountain and back, I was at a loss. "It doesn't seem like your style…" I ventured.

"No, no," he replied, waving his hand. "I forgot, you wouldn't know, you haven't met him. Mick's here! Set pieces with fire were always his thing. Fantastic in the winter."

A surprise reappearance of an old friend: that made sense. Out of nowhere, a tiny part of my brain registered something like disappointment that I hadn't been the one to raise his spirits like this, but I quickly tamped that down, wondering what the hell I was thinking. "Is he… back? Sticking around, I mean, or is this just a cameo appearance?"

"Just for a couple of days. He usually tries to drop in when we're within striking distance, but he can't often get away for a whole stay anywhere."

"He wasn't at Callanish, though, was he?" I asked.

Eric shook his head. "His wife had appendicitis. Poor bastard was devastated to miss it. Look, we're just going to see Gavin's act – come and join us?"

Belatedly, I remembered where I had intended to be. "I was just on my way to go and see Claire. Can I meet you later? I haven't missed your show, have I?"

"Not yet." He grinned at me. "Although if I'd known Mick was coming, I would have gone on earlier so I could go drink with him after. I'm starting around twelve-thirty, maybe a little sooner. See you then?"

"If not before."

Claire's performance went ahead without incident, and without any need for her to flee into the night. Catching up with her outside, I suspected she might not be in the mood for further confidences, so instead I asked her if she knew Mick.

"Not really," she said, pursing her lips. "Everyone knows *of* him, and has met him here and there, but it's been a while since he was a regular part of the troupe. He and Gavin and Eric have always been thick as thieves, though."

"Why did he leave?"

She shrugged. "It was before my time. He's married, but I don't know if that had to do with it or if they met later." It seemed like conversation was not high on her list of priorities, and clearly the best way to find out more about this Mick character was to go and meet him myself. I wandered through the field, down some of the smaller, less orderly aisles of tents. There was a decent wind blowing in from the west, ushering a parade of clouds across the waning moon – mirrored at ground level by the dance of light and shadow as tents opened, disgorged crowds of people, went dark. I was just beginning to think it must be nearly time to go find Eric's marquee, when I spotted Gavin, illuminated by a stray burst from somewhere.

I saw him in profile, in animated conversation with a man I had not seen before. The stranger was on the shorter side, with a spare frame, standing very still. When I drew closer, he looked a couple of days unshaven - deliberately so, if I had to guess - with a shock of short dark hair just barely tinged with grey round the temples. Despite the cold weather, he had no jacket, just a khaki sweater over his stovepipe jeans.

My intent was to observe discreetly, but Gavin caught my eye and motioned me over. When the stranger turned my way, I was struck by his eyes, almost too large for his face. I couldn't decide if he was handsome or not. "And this is Heather," Gavin declared, as if I were the concluding argument in a case. "Newly joined us.

Heather Ross: Mick Rutherford."

Mick fixed me with his overlarge gaze and repeated my name. "I've heard a great deal about you."

He eyed me up and down, not troubling to hide the fact that he was doing so, or giving away any hints of what he thought. There was a distinct haze of alcohol around the both of them, but I supposed one could make some allowances for the prodigal's return. "I hear that a lot these days."

Silence fell for a moment, before Gavin clapped us both on the shoulders and announced it was time we went to see Eric. As it had been the first time I saw it, Eric's tent was the deepest of greens, only distinguishable from black when the light hit it in a slow pulse, an emerald heartbeat against the night. We joined the crowd filing in – Mick and Gavin still talking amongst themselves in low voices – and found seats at the perimeter, where the mist was not as heavy. Something about that unnatural fog always seemed to quiet a crowd, and in the general hush even my companions saw fit to end their discussion.

A sound began: barely noticeable at first, but deepening to a clear, bell-like tone that came out of nowhere. The echoes of the note hung in the air as the mist began to coalesce into shapes. Eric's performances were a little different every time, but even so, it took me by surprise when a dragon – deep green like the silks surrounding us – materialized at the centre of the ring. Its fiery breath could have been mistaken for real, if it were not for the fact that it cast no heat. It was followed by a series of other fantastic, nearly lifelike beasts: unicorns, griffins, minotaurs, and others I would have been hard pressed to put a name to. Some of them lunged at the audience, eliciting gasps and shrieks as they circled the tent.

The last illusion was the most compelling. A long, lithe shape split into three: a trio of werewolves prowling the room, every feature of their faces clearly detailed, resting on the knife-point balance between human and animal. When one of them passed close by me, I couldn't help a gasp as it looked my way; I felt as if I were staring into a real face, depths of wisdom and wildness as the figure's gaze met mine. Just when I was beginning to wonder what might come next, the three merged into one dark-pelted wolf. It stood on its hind legs at the centre of the ring, then slowly the mist dropped away to show instead Eric Heyward, all in black.

The audience seemed to need a split-second to assure themselves that the performance was at an end and that this was indeed a flesh-and-blood man before them — but then, as one, they burst into applause as he took his bow. And then with one final burst of vapour, he disappeared: an extra flourish I had not seen before.

I sat a while, listening to the enthusiastic reactions of the patrons as they filed out of the tent, but when I realized that Gavin and Mick had gone as well, I set out to find my vanished friend.

CHAPTER EIGHT

A few tents stood scattered around the fringe of the field, tucked out of sight of the average visitor, where three old friends might opt to spend a little downtime. It took some looking, but when I eventually stumbled on a little square midnight-blue marquee, I could hear the laughter even from outdoors.

Inside, it was more spacious than it had appeared, with a small fire crackling in a stone dish atop a scarred wooden table. Mick was holding court at the head of the table, clearly partway through a many-times-told anecdote, with Eric and Gavin finishing his sentences here and there. Around the table, and on benches at the side, sat many of the younger magicians, drawn in by this novelty in their midst.

"He's never set foot here, mind," Mick was saying. "But he's related. His dad was a cousin of... who was it?"

"Cousin of Arthur's dad, wasn't it?" Gavin supplied.

Mick shook his head. "Nah, I think it was somebody in Raffaele's line. Least that's what I've heard. Don't you give me that look, Heyward."

Eric rolled his eyes. "You're full of shit. You've been telling this story since the eighties. Until he drops by and does a trick for us, I'm not believing he's a magician, or half a magician or quarter-magician or whatever."

"Well, it might be a few generations back," Mick allowed.

"Go back far enough and probably half of the world's got some tiny, tiny percentage of magician blood," Eric retorted, demonstrating by holding his thumb and forefinger perhaps a hair's-breadth apart, before picking up his beer again and taking a sip. "You're reaching."

Another shake of the head. "Riddle me this, then," Mick said, getting to his feet. "How's he still alive? If he hasn't got some bit of magic in those veins, working against everything else?"

The argument was clearly one that had been waged before: younger faces hung on every word, others were warming to a familiar theme. Looking around, I spotted Luke and edged over to him. "Who are they talking about, anyhow?" I asked in an undertone, as his other companions turned away.

He leaned in to reply. "Keith Richards."

"You've got to be kidding me." When I thought about it, though, it was far from the strangest thing I had seen or heard in recent months. Who knew; perhaps that was indeed his secret?

The argument fizzled out while I considered this. "Heather, come join us," Eric said, waving me over. Spectacle concluded, the onlookers wandered out or went back to their own drinks, leaving me with the three men. I didn't want to interfere with their little reunion, and said so, but Eric insisted, moving over to clear some room on the bench. Gavin smiled at me, but I thought Mick was decidedly less pleased. He covered it well, though, and set to asking me questions about myself: pleasant enough on the surface, but I felt as if I were in a job interview, or maybe the principal's office.

"And you really never had any idea?" he asked, when the inquiries inevitably led around to the topic of my family tree. I had only known of my descent from Raffaele and Sébastien for a few short months and I was already growing heartily sick of hearing about them.

"You were born into this." I didn't bother to make it a question; I had found that incomers like Eric and Eleanor were much less obsessed with the question of lineage. "And you left. For the most part," I added, gesturing to the basin of fire, and at him sitting there. "Did you have any idea – as a child, as a teenager – that you were going to do that?"

Mick raised one eyebrow. "Touché. No, I never thought I'd stray. But with art, I can make something that endures. This is ephemeral – for all it keeps us old bastards looking presentable." He narrowed his eyes a little. "And I fell in love with a woman I can trust. You have to be careful who you trust, here."

"Heather, what are you drinking? Let me grab you one," Gavin interjected, a little too obviously. I wondered what Mick was getting at.

I shook my head. "You know what? I'm going to get some fresh air. You guys catch up," I added, when Eric looked like he was going to say something. "I'll be back in a bit."

As I wandered away down the row of tents, I heard footsteps coming up from behind and realized that Eric had followed me. Some small part of me was gratified by it, though I knew I shouldn't be. "Don't do that," I groaned. "This is supposed to be your chance to catch up with Mick. Go on – I don't think he likes me very much as it is." It was one of those things that I hadn't realized I was thinking until it popped out of my mouth. "I don't want to make it worse."

"Don't take him the wrong way," he replied, shaking his head. "He turns the spotlight on you; it's just how he is with new people. It's not personal."

"Alright," I replied, unconvinced, waving him back in the direction of the tent. "But go back in there. I promise I'll come back and join you in a little while, if you want. I'm going to go for a walk in the glen. If I'm gone more than an hour, send a search party," I joked, in response to his expression.

Patting him on the arm, I turned towards the darkness at the outside of the carnival, wondering whether what I really wanted was for him to follow me.

Given that, just the night before, I had been worried about Claire being followed out to the glen, I did take just a second to wonder whether I should be going off on my own. If nothing else, the night had clouded over and become about as dark as the inside of a closet. Taking that into consideration, I stayed down on the ground rather than attempting to scale the rock outcrop. I found a dryish patch of grass — somewhere near the stone labyrinth pattern, by my estimation — and sat down, my hands to the earth, reaching out with my senses to try and get a better understanding of the magic that this place possessed.

When I heard voices, I thought I might have disturbed somebody else, or perhaps I only hoped that I had. After a few seconds, I heard someone so close at hand that I started to my feet, heart racing. They were speaking French, I thought: a masculine voice, low and vaguely familiar. Another voice answered; this one I was certain I had heard, but could not place.

My French had never been tremendously fluent, and it had been a long time since I'd used it, but still, I understood what the first voice said next. "Elle nous écoute." *She is listening to us.*

"Who's there?" I asked, trying to sound braver than I felt.

"Do you not know your own flesh and blood?" the first voice replied, a distinct accent remaining as he switched to English. *Truly, do you not?*

45

The question was repeated inside my head, not outside. My eyes searched the darkness till they ached, but there was no one to be seen. "You're not Desrochers." His voice I would have recognized, I was sure.

"No, indeed I am not."

Which left only one option. I was surprised I hadn't come upon it straight away. "Sébastien." At any other time in my life prior to the last few months, hearing the voice of a dead man I'd never met would have been a bad dream as the best-case scenario. Now, it almost seemed as though I should have been expecting this. "Why are you here?"

"I have always been here." I wondered if he meant the Fairy Glen, or inside my head. Either way, he sounded amused; I had no doubt it was at my expense. "I have had my share of descendants; very few of them have inherited the gift. Fewer still have taken full possession of it."

"And so you're speaking to me because I have?"

He chuckled, the sound outside my head rather than inside, though I wondered if it would have been audible to anyone else. "Let us not get ahead of ourselves. You are not quite there yet."

He still hadn't really answered my question. "And you're here to teach me, then?"

A vague sound, the verbal equivalent of a shrug. Although I wasn't sure I wanted his guidance – I wasn't sure I even wanted to be talking to him – it annoyed me. "You taught Raffaele." Then I remembered the second voice. "Raffaele? Are you here too?"

"He was. He has gone, for now. He took an enormous interest in you, given your brief acquaintance. I wonder what would have happened if I had let him have Christiane, rather than their offspring meeting by chance and letting the gift languish three generations. Their child might have been truly remarkable; I see that now."

His tone of idle interest struck me as repellent. "Were you always a complete ass, or did that come with the magic?"

Sébastien actually laughed. "I was not a virtuous man, nor an evil one. Simply a man, with greater means at my disposal than most. Not bulletproof, alas." He paused. "Raffaele was right; you are of some interest. You are resilient, like the scrubby little weed they named you for. You have self-taught a great deal in a short time, and have been shrewd enough to ally yourself with the Kavanaghs, which has brought you status and protection beyond the typical newcomer. And you mastered mindspeaking when my idiot child confronted you, even if all of you grossly overestimated the threat he posed, lunatic that he is. Kavanagh's bastard might have killed him with his bare hands, given the chance. It might have been a mercy, truly. But I am making a digression. I am here because I am curious."

I had no idea where to begin with his strange take on my last few months, so I asked the obvious question. "About what?"

"You are a mindspeaker. The first in a generation, perhaps longer. You know this, and can direct it with purpose. So why do you not use it?"

"I haven't needed to. I hope I never need to use it again."

"Why?"

Having a feeling it would fall on deaf ears, I answered regardless. "I can't think of many situations where it's justifiable. Other than self-defense. It may be handy to know how to throw a knockout punch, too, but you can't just walk down the street punching people in the face because you feel like it."

As soon as I said it, it occurred to me that I was talking to a person who quite possibly would have found appeal in going around punching people for sheer entertainment. However, rather than amused, he sounded vaguely annoyed when he replied. "Morality. It is a tiresome thing. I see you are burdened with it."

"You may not have cared what people thought of you," I said, feeling that I was stating the obvious, "but I've been on the receiving end of being betrayed. I couldn't do that to someone. How could anyone trust me, if I went around influencing people's minds?"

"If they are aware enough to mistrust you, you are doing it wrong. It can be a subtle tool as well as a blacksmith's hammer. Do you think any of them spoke ill of me in my lifetime? I was held in high regard: loved, even. If the veil lifted from their eyes when I was gone, that is hardly my concern. You hold riches in your hand and throw them away. Think what you can do, if you only choose to use your legacy. Cease Isabella's grousing against you. Cause audiences to fall at your feet and shower you with gifts. Make your handsome husband forget his mistresses and come back to you, if you like. Or… perhaps there is something else you would choose? Interesting."

"Get out of my head!"

"You know perfectly well that that idea was of your own making and not mine," he replied, chuckling to himself. "Now that you know your talent, you will always be able to distinguish another mindspeaker's voice from your own."

My cheeks flushed red, at the image that had sprung into my mind and at the fact that Sébastien had seen it and found it entertaining. "If you have anything useful to say, say it. Otherwise…"

He laughed once more. "What will you do, to a dead man? Think on what I have said. We will talk again."

The last words faded away, like smoke in the wind, and I knew that our conversation was at an end.

Still fuming, I stalked away.

Or rather, I stalked perhaps twenty steps – not paying particular attention where I was going in my haste to get away from my ancestor's voice – before I lost my footing in some kind of hole. My ankle rolled to one side and I fell heavily, my right hip hitting a rock. Cursing under my breath, I considered my stupidity at having wandered off into the dark in the first place. I was used to the dangers that came with city life, and not rabbit burrows on a moonless night. Given my surroundings, I supposed that I was lucky I hadn't hit my head, but trying to stand up did not give me great confidence in my ability to make it back to the tents under my own power. After hobbling a little ways, I sat down again and considered my options.

My phone didn't get reception out in the glen – even at the hostel, it was hit and miss – but it could at least tell me that it was a little past two in the morning. Dawn was ages away. Rolling up the leg of my jeans, I felt the injured area. I could move my foot around – uncomfortably, but without stabbing pain – and I didn't think anything was broken, but it was already beginning to swell. The road was only a short distance away, so if I could use my phone as a light to carefully pick my way along, I would reach a more stable walking surface.

Determined to make the best of it, I got to my feet, used my phone's flashlight for some feeble illumination, and gingerly stepped forward. My foot held my weight, which was a relief, but it was going to be a long way to hobble all the way back to the carnival. Getting back to the hostel on foot didn't bear thinking about.

I was about halfway to the road when I heard a familiar voice off to my left – a welcome one, this time. "Heather?"

"Over here," I called, waving my phone. "What are you doing here?" I asked, as Eric jogged over.

"It's been over an hour; you said to send a search party," he joked, then looked more closely at me in the dim electronic light. "What's wrong?"

"Twisted my ankle. I was just trying to figure out whether I'd make it back under my own steam, but I am very glad to see you. Thanks," I added, as he put his arm around me to help. "But that's not even the half of it."

"Why, what else happened?"

"I'm okay," I began, hearing the concern in his voice. "Apart from the ankle, I'm not hurt or anything otherwise. But… It's a long story. It's weird."

"I'd expect nothing less," he said, joking again. "Let's get you to a comfortable chair and an ice pack, and then you can spill the details."

Most of them, I thought.

CHAPTER NINE

When we reached the road, I found walking a little easier, as long as I could lean on Eric's arm, and so I suggested we just head back to the hostel. "There's no point hiking over there," I said, nodding my head in the vague direction of the tents, "and then just retracing our steps later. I don't think anyone's in any state to drive tonight, even if they had a car handy."

"True. Just let me know if you need to take a break."

After that, we carried on in silence; I was concentrating on soldiering ahead despite the pain in my ankle. "Sorry to tear you away from the guys," I said eventually, when we finally came out of the country lane to the main road, within sight of our destination. "I guess you don't get to see Mick very often."

"Nah, it's okay." I could smell the tang of beer on his breath, and woodsmoke clung to his jacket. "He's going to stick around for a couple of days, I think. Jesus, you really are white as a sheet," he added, as we came into a pool of light at the end of the driveway. "Good thing we're nearly there."

The last incline up the drive did make me feel a little queasy, and I gratefully slumped down onto the first couch in the common room once we got inside. What would normally have been about a twenty-five-minute walk had taken us well over an hour, and once I managed to get my shoes off I saw that my ankle seemed to have puffed up to twice its normal size. "Delightful."

"I've seen worse," he replied, pulling up a spare chair for me to rest my foot on before heading into the kitchen to scrounge up a makeshift ice pack. "You might want to stay off it for a day or two, though. No dish washing or security patrolling or whatever other odd jobs you feel compelled to do," he added, before I could respond.

"I just want to be helpful."

"We all pitch in, yeah. But you don't have to do some kind of..." He waved his hand around vaguely. "I don't know, penance or something, to earn the right to perform, especially if it's just because Isabella has convinced some of the others to have a beef with you." Shaking his head, he sat down beside me.

I tried to turn to look at him, as best I could without jostling my leg. "Why does it bug you so much?"

He shrugged. "I feel like you're getting punished for what happened in Germany. You're the one that talked to Sofia, so I don't know, but it just seems like people are getting the wrong idea. You're the victim here, not the bad guy. But hey, you were supposed to tell me what happened in the glen."

I considered how to explain it, and eventually decided that the direct approach was best. "I heard voices in the dark, and wound up having a lengthy conversation with Sébastien. I know how that sounds," I added, when Eric didn't respond right away.

"I don't think you're crazy. Weird things happen out there at night. And it almost seems like he was bound to show up sometime."

I let out a breath I hadn't realized I'd been holding. "You know, I'd almost forgotten, but I'd thought that too. I had half-expected to meet him when I did the Magician's Walk." And then I thought back to the one presence that night that I had not seen, only heard. "I'm wondering now if maybe I did."

Silence fell for several moments, and I knew Eric must be thinking about who else I had seen in the Black Forest that night. I wasn't sure how to recover the conversation, but after a while he spoke again. "What did he look like? I don't think I've ever heard anyone describe him, appearance-wise."

"It was just his voice. I never saw anything." Suddenly, I wondered if any photos of him existed. "He was talking to someone at first. To Raffaele, but he… left, I guess, when I heard them and spoke up. They were speaking French, but he switched to English to talk to me."

I recounted the conversation – much of it verbatim, as it was certainly still fresh in my mind. When I came to Sébastien's assessment of the fracas in Germany, I paused. "He didn't seem to think Desrochers really posed much of a threat. I don't know if that's because he's crazy – Desrochers, that is – or because I could use the same ability…"

"Mindspeaking," Eric supplied. When I made a dismissive noise, he continued. "It's a decent enough name for it, and I bet he didn't coin the term, if that makes you feel any better. I mean, I don't know any history of… this…" He waved a hand. "At least any further back than things I've heard from Ben, and from Daniel and Molly. And I know Sébastien supposedly wasn't descended from any other magicians, but he can't have been the first person of all time to have that skill. Even he said – what was it, that you were the first in a generation? So it's rare. But it cannot have started, full-fledged, with him. I refuse to believe that. But sorry… go on."

I tried to remember where I had been going with my sentence, then thought of the next thing Sébastien had said to me. "He thought you might have killed Desrochers. 'Given the chance', as he put it."

The question in my mind must have been clear, because that was what Eric answered. "Honestly? My memory of that night is a bit weird. I know he was manipulating me – although I obviously couldn't tell at the time – and it was as if those spaces of time I was drunk, and then instantly sober as soon as he stopped focusing on me. I'm probably not explaining it well. I admit, when I had control of my faculties, my only thought was to get him out of the picture by any means necessary. But would I have killed him? I don't think so. I hope not. If it had meant saving your life..." His eyes met mine, just for a second, and I could see the rest of that thought. "Thankfully," he added, "you had that situation under control. You rescued yourself. And maybe it's true that he's just a nutjob. But it was satisfying to punch that asshole, and I would do *that* again without thinking twice." He grinned, the tension suddenly gone. "It seems weird that I've heard all these stories about Sébastien, and then he's talking about me by name."

"Well," I said slowly. "Not exactly." I recounted how Sébastien had referred to him, trying not to put too much weight on the words. "He was very interested in how – as he saw it – I'd cleverly allied myself with the whole Kavanagh family, when in fact they've sort of adopted me, mainly thanks to you. He's incredibly Machiavellian. And I think he thinks that it goes hand in hand with the ability – the mindspeaking. He seemed to assume that because I have the talent, that I'd also have the same mindset, at least to a point. He was quite disappointed in me that I don't want to use it for my own ends. He even gave me a sales pitch."

"What do you mean?"

"He... basically said I could get whatever I wanted: that I could make Isabella like me, have audiences falling at my feet, that I could have Alan back. Not that I would want him," I added, rolling my eyes.

"Is that the first time you've told me your ex's name?" Eric asked. "I don't remember."

"Alan. Alan Ridout. Happy?" I didn't want to talk about my ex-husband. Although I had to admit, his entry into the topics of conversation had neatly sidestepped the part I wanted to talk about even less – the thought that had amused Sébastien, the thing that had popped into my head completely unbidden when he had tried to entice me into exploiting the legacy he'd passed on. "As if one underhanded scumbag wasn't enough to be talking about at... what is it now, four in the morning?"

Eric pulled out his phone and glanced at it. "Nearly. Look, I'm still curious about this whole experience, and if you want to talk more about it I'm not going anywhere. But you should probably get some sleep if you want to be back on your feet any time soon."

Part of me wanted to keep hashing things out – to try to make more sense of it all – but another part was very tired indeed. "I'm going to call it a night. Maybe I'll have some epiphany about all of this by daylight."

By the next morning, I had no particular flashes of insight, and my ankle was black-and-blue and still swollen. I could hobble around, but it was clear that I wasn't going very far. Fortunately, 'twisted my foot in a rabbit hole' sufficed for the couple of people who noticed, and no one asked any awkward questions about what I'd been doing in the glen on my own in the pitch black. I was making some toast, leaning against the counter with my weight mostly on my good side, when Gavin came round to the kitchen and gave me the once-over. "You sure you shouldn't have that looked at?"

"Can't really do that. I'm not on the NHS over here," I pointed out. It was one of the first things that had occurred to me after the injury – something that I knew I'd have to sort out at some point, if I was going to come to this side of the pond to live, but for the moment that was neither here nor there.

He waved his hand carelessly. "My cousin works in the sport clinic in town. I'll text her and get her to give it a look. I've got to go do a supply run anyhow."

"Are you sure?"

He took his keys from his pocket. "Go on, get your things."

My dormmates were still asleep, so I left a note on Eleanor's bag saying where I'd gone, and hobbled out to Gavin's car. Where the driveway met the road, he put on his left turn indicator, then turned it off again. "Have you been to Skye before?"

"Technically, but I didn't get much further than Kyleakin," I replied. "It was one of those backpacker bus tour things, years ago when I was still in university. Why?"

He shrugged, and put the right-hand signal on, before turning out of the driveway in the direction of the village. "Just thought we'd take the scenic route round, then, if that's alright with you."

After passing around the curve at the end of the bay, the road narrowed to a single track and rose steeply out of Uig before emerging into countryside. Hilly grazing land rolled down to the Atlantic and the vague smudge of Harris and Lewis could be seen near the horizon.

"Your... cousin," I ventured, after a few minutes. "Does your whole family live around here?"

"Most of them. Buying the hostel is a bit of a homecoming for me. I'm not the only magician, though," he added, answering my real question. "And it's not a big secret. I know it probably seems like an all or nothing proposition, but it's kind of skipped around in our gene pool. Jeannie Mac, the one who teaches the kids, is my first cousin, and her dad – you probably won't have met him – he's still sitting in with the elders, but doesn't perform so often anymore. Our granny taught Daniel and Molly Kavanagh when they were just wee kids, at the turn of the last century. But Granny married out – a non-magician, that is. He was a music hall singer from the King's Theatre in Glasgow who saw her act and fell for her straight away, as the story goes. So we're a bit of a mixed bag. My dad was a kid here – with the carnival – and doesn't have a lick of magic. I grew up in Greenock and didn't know the family history till I was twelve, when I fell out of a tree one day and landed like a feather instead of a ton of bricks. I guess Dad figured then that he'd best put me in touch with my roots. We started coming round during the school holidays, till I left home at seventeen to join up properly. The rest is history, I guess."

I pondered this, thinking of how much I still had to learn about this community I'd joined. "So… your grandfather came to live with the troupe, as a non-magician? How does that sort of thing work?"

He glanced over at me, one eyebrow raised. "Why, have you got someone in mind?" he teased, before carrying on. "By the time I started visiting Granny with the troupe, instead of her always coming south to see us, my granddad was already gone, so I can't say in their case. But it happens. Not everybody with us now is a magician, you know. Some of them travel with us all the time, some are back home and join us when they can. For people with kids, it sometimes depends whether they think the kids have the gift; if so, it's more likely that the whole family will come along."

"And some people find a non-magic partner and leave. Like Mick, right?"

"It was the art that took him away, really. It might have done, even if he hadn't met Anna."

I wondered what she was like; I couldn't quite picture him with a wife. "Does she know?"

"That he's a magician?" Gavin replied. "Yeah, of course. It's one thing to hide it from someone you go with for a while, but that'd be a big skeleton to keep in the closet for that long. So really, why all the questions? From what I've heard, I don't think you'd be planning to bring your ex out here, and I didn't get the sense that Mick made a big impression on you."

For a few moments, I just looked out the window, debating my answer. "Just realizing how much I don't actually know about all this. Trying to figure out how it all works."

He laughed. "Oh, I think you'll find not many have that totally figured out."

The drive truly was the scenic route, encompassing a ruined castle, waterfalls, and several of the stunning landforms that I had only previously seen on postcards. By the time we neared Portree, the closest thing to a sizable town, it was past lunchtime. A check in with Gavin's cousin the doctor – who refused to take any form of payment despite my efforts to offer something – confirmed that what I had was a mild sprain.

"You should be feeling more like yourself in a week or so," she advised. "Less, if you're anything like the rest of Gavin's lot, but don't go doing any running or sport for a while, till the New Year at least. Rest it up today and tomorrow, keep it elevated when you can, and ice it a few times. After that, just use your judgment and don't overdo."

Gavin had gone off to run errands; on his return, he insisted that we stop in a nearby pub for something to eat. "So, now it's my turn to ask you some questions," he began, once he returned from making our order at the bar, bearing a cider for me and what looked like orange soda for himself.

Not without some apprehension, I nodded. "Okay."

"What do you – or did you, before you decided to throw your lot in with us – do for work?"

I blinked, not having expected such a conventional question. "Outreach and fundraising, mostly. I was working for a non-profit, but some grants dried up and they had to lay me off about a year and a half ago. Same day I caught my ex cheating and threw him out, in fact."

"Quite a day."

"Indeed. Then I did some contract and freelance stuff for a while. Why do you ask?"

Gavin took a sip of his drink. "You don't happen to know how to do websites and that, do you?"

I held one hand up and wavered it. "On a small scale, I've done a bit of that kind of thing. Why? If you need a website for the hostel, surely there are other people you could ask."

"You'll be needing some kind of thing to do, in between travelling," he answered, his tone casual. "And if I can give you a good review, that might swing some weight with someone who does have some more substantial work that needs done."

I sat back against the bench, thoroughly confused by the whole line of discussion. "And... that would be...?"

He looked pleased with himself. "Mick, of course. And Eric, if he moves up to help Mick run his art centre. Which of course he will, eventually. Especially if it's true what I hear, that you're thinking of staying somewhere around there yourself. If you're not going to be an artist, or start a business yourself, then it makes sense to work for another magician, aye?"

There would be a certain sort of odd logic in that, if not for one thing. "Mick doesn't like me."

"Well," Gavin said slowly, screwing up his face a little, "it's not that he doesn't like you. He takes a while to warm up to new people. And..."

"And what?"

"It's just… The three of us, Eric and Mick and me, we've known each other for twenty-five years, and we've all made more than our share of absolutely terrible decisions, suffered through them, and helped each other pick up the pieces. We've done a lot of stupid shit, together and separately. But nothing – nothing – was as consistently, interminably fucking toxic and self-destructive like Eric and Stasia together."

I still wasn't sure why he was telling me this. "And they were together a long time."

He nodded. "And it's water under the bridge – ages ago – but there's a certain protectiveness there still, I guess. I mean, don't tell him I said any of this, or he'd have my guts for garters," he added, with a bit of a laugh. "And I'm making no assumptions, but you know, Mick's missed your whole appearance on the scene and everything that's happened since, and all he knows is that Heyward's spending practically all his time with the new magician who just happens to be female, American…"

"Canadian," I corrected.

"Close enough." He waved his hand carelessly. "How far's Toronto from where he's from – like Edinburgh to Glasgow?"

I sat back, arms folded, and let the geographical details fall by the wayside. "And does he give this sort of treatment to every woman that crosses Eric's path?"

"Heyward doesn't let many get close. We don't see as much of what goes on when we're not travelling, but I wouldn't be surprised if you're the first in ten years."

"Bullshit. What about Eleanor, for starters?"

"Not the same. And it wasn't her that he went out of his way to meet up with first, when he came back after his dad."

It hadn't been Gavin, either, and I wondered for a moment whether that had stung a little. He was one who I still didn't quite have a read on, and our conversation was not doing much to illuminate me. But he carried on. "And to top it off with all the… excitement, shall we say, around your roots and all. And - you know, the Germany thing. All I'm saying is, don't take it too personally if Mick comes off a bit abrasive."

"I'll try."

By the time we finally made it back to the hostel it was already dark, and my ankle was protesting the amount of time spent sitting in the car. I found a chair where I could prop my foot up, and accepted gratefully when Gavin offered to fix up an icepack. He was just helping me get comfortably settled with it, when I felt the sensation of eyes boring into my skull. I looked up to see Eric silhouetted in the doorway, but only for a moment. Without a word to either of us, he turned and walked out.

"What the hell was that?" I muttered, more to myself than anything. Gavin heard it, though, and to my surprise he looked almost pleased.

"Don't worry about it. He'll get over himself in his own time." He offered no further insight, and indeed it was time for him – and all the others – to be heading out for the evening's festivities. It irked me that I could not simply stomp off after Eric and find out what had him in such a mood.

Gavin excused himself and joined a group of people filing out the door. Eventually, the building grew silent and it seemed that I was the only one left. I took advantage of the unusual quiet to write a letter to my gran, peruse a few chapters of a paperback novel someone had left in the common room, and then headed off to bed at the sort of hour that I had formerly thought of as a 'normal' bedtime. Lying on the thin mattress of my bunk, I stared up into the dark for a while, wondering what was happening out by the glen, before eventually drifting off into sleep.

My dreams were full of mixed-up images: people's faces blurring into each other, Eric turning into Mick turning into Sofia the oracle, talking about the shadow hanging over me as I struggled to navigate my way through a place that was somehow simultaneously a field of tents, and my old high school. Just as I was trying to execute a difficult piece of illusion in front of my grade-ten math teacher, I awoke suddenly to find the night well advanced, the silence buffered by the quiet sound of other sleepers' breathing. The show was over for the night, then.

I was on the cusp of falling back asleep when I realized something was a bit off. My brain registered the weight at the end of the bed, but took a while to connect the dots to the fact that someone was sitting there, down by my feet.

The room was so dark that I could barely distinguish a thing, even when I lifted my head and opened my eyes fully, but my movement must have demonstrated that I was awake. There was a muttered curse, followed by an apology.

"Eric?" I hissed, under my breath. "What the hell are you doing?"

"I'm sorry," he repeated, seeming like he was aiming to be a little quieter than he actually was. He said it again, in a lower tone. "Sorry. I just… wanted to talk to you."

He was drunk; that much was clear. I could smell the alcohol on him, even if his clumsy speech hadn't told the tale. I doubted he was going to make a lot of sense. "It's late. You're going to wake everyone up. Can we talk in the morning?"

"Right. Yes. You're right. I'm sorry."

I put my head back on the pillow. "It's fine. Go to bed, we'll talk later."

He obliged, thankfully managing to exit the room without making much noise. Closing my eyes, I thought *what the hell?* again, before drifting back to sleep.

CHAPTER TEN

I woke up into a vaguely daylit room, the morning already well advanced, though none of my bunkmates were yet stirring. I could almost have convinced myself that Eric's strange visit had been just another dream. Almost.

Padding through the quiet building towards the kitchen – if nothing else, my ankle did seem improved – I considered what on earth he had been thinking, coming to my room in the middle of the night. For starters, I hadn't even realized he had known what room I was in, let alone figuring out which was my bunk in an inebriated state. His reaction when I'd woken up suggested that he'd had the good sense to think better of the idea. As for what he'd wanted to talk to me about, I had to assume that it was some kind of explanation for his cryptic behaviour earlier in the evening.

The first person I saw stirring was Ari. He didn't seem to notice that anyone else was up until he had already retrieved a tin of pop from the fridge. "Didn't see you there," he said, blinking at me.

"Did I miss anything exciting last night?"

He shrugged. "Not too much to report, except that Mick's still here, and he's always a loose cannon." Ari was not the sort to give away much with his facial expressions, but his tone suggested that he could do without loose cannons. "Seemed like he and Eric and Gavin were having words at some point towards the end, but as long as no one comes to blows, I'm not bothered." With that, he drifted away.

I filed that last bit of information away for further consideration. Left to my own devices, I propped my bad foot up on a spare chair and was about to resume the novel I'd left on the table the night before, when I noticed voices coming from Gavin's end of the building. A few moments later, he and Mick emerged, not seeming to notice anything else as they crossed to the front door and exited. Tension was obvious in both their postures, though whether it was directed at each other I couldn't tell. From where I was sitting, I could see about half of the yard out the front window; Gavin paced around for a few minutes while Mick smoked a cigarette, then they drove off.

It was time to find out what was going on, decency be damned. There was no one to notice or care that I headed into the old cottage instead of towards the dorms, and it was just as well that I found the door unlocked, as I hadn't really considered the alternative. The couch in the front room was half-covered in a disarrayed blanket, but empty, and the doors to the bathroom and kitchen stood open, revealing no signs of life. Of the two remaining doors, I knew the one on the right led to Gavin's bedroom; I tried the left.

The room was small, not enough space for much more than the single futon on the floor that was its only furnishing. Without curtains, there was enough grey light to see the clothes carelessly dropped on the carpet, the faded chevron pattern on the duvet, and the tousled head half-visible above the covers.

I drew the line at perching on the mattress. Gingerly, I lowered myself down to sit on the floor where I could lean my back against the wall. Given the way Eric had startled me overnight, I didn't feel particularly bad about waking him up. Reaching out a hand – careful to keep it on top of the duvet, as I had no idea how dressed he might be underneath – I jostled his shoulder, none too carefully. "Hey."

"Hmmf? Heather?" His voice changed as he woke up more fully, and he repeated my name, raising himself up on one elbow and blinking at me in obvious confusion. "Shit. Sorry about last night."

So I hadn't mixed up dreams and reality, then. "I think you need to tell me what the hell is going on."

When he sat up, I was relieved to see he had a t-shirt on. "Yeah. I think I'd better."

He pressed his fingers against his temples for a few seconds, then ran his hands through his hair, clearly trying to wake up a bit more. "I'm sorry about sneaking up on you like that last night," he repeated. "That was ridiculously inappropriate. You know… have you ever had the thing where you have too much to drink, and like a complete fool you think something needs to get said or done right away? I tried to text you to see if you were up, but of course there's no reception…"

"Trust me, I've done stuff like that too. What was it that you needed to talk to me about so badly?"

There was a long pause, making me wonder if he was having second thoughts about whatever had seemed so pressing a few hours before. "First off, I'm sorry I walked out earlier in the evening."

"Yeah, what was that about, anyhow?"

"Like I said, impulsive stuff, that doesn't make sense when I take a second to think about it. I guess I got a bit bent out of shape when you disappeared with Gavin for the day. I know, I know," he added, holding up his hands to prevent me interrupting. "Let me just fill you in on the rest of it."

"Go on."

He took a deep breath. "Mick's been giving me the third degree about you, almost since he got here. At first it was just, you know, the usual shit." His gaze was on the duvet as he spoke, and it could have just been the hangover and the lack of sleep, but I thought his cheeks had gone slightly pink. I knew what sort of assumptions people made about us – almost since the moment we'd met – and I could well imagine that Mick might have characterized those ideas less than delicately.

"Hope he doesn't walk in, then," I said, trying for a light tone but knowing I sounded sarcastic.

"Yeah. But… here's the thing. He's got this idea into his head now, since he inevitably heard Luke's stories about what happened in Germany, that…"

"What?"

"That you can't be trusted. Not because of what Desrochers did, but because of how you handled it. Because you've got Sébastien's gift. The – what did he call it? Mindspeaking."

"What?" I repeated. "I did it once, when I thought I was in danger. Well, twice. But he thinks…?" And then my tirade halted, as the full impact of the idea hit me. "He thinks I'll use it all the time."

"I told him that's bullshit. You're not Sébastien."

"For all he knows, I might be." One hand over my mouth, I let those words echo in my head, as several puzzle pieces shifted and fell into place in my mind's eye. Every magician in the company knew what had happened at Bad Dürkheim – if not every single detail, certainly the general shape of things, and probably a little distorted by hearsay – and several of them had witnessed it first-hand. It was no secret that I had at least some command of 'mindspeaking', as my unsavoury ancestor had called it. "For all most of them know. Most of them know fuck-all about me."

"So what? Okay, so Mick just showed up, but he's still out of line. You've done nothing to justify anyone doubting you."

"As far as they know." Because truly, that was the crux of it: if I could mindspeak like Sébastien, then how could anyone trust anything? Sébastien had made people think the way he wanted, do things he wanted them to do. He had used his mind tricks to seduce countless women, and there was no knowing to what other ends he had applied his disturbing talent. Everyone knew that I had inherited the skill, and if I were ever to develop it beyond the faint inkling I already possessed, then I would be the only one to ever know for sure whether the people around me were acting of their own free will. Shadow hanging over my head, indeed.

Eric put a hand around my wrist, forcing me to uncover my face. "Heather. He's full of shit."

"Actually, he's not."

"Uh-huh. Have you ever used it on anybody besides Desrochers?"

About to say no, I thought of Isabella turning and walking away on the first night of the show. "Not that I know of."

"And when you did use it, was it easy?"

"Easy? No. I could barely make a dent in him."

"Exactly," he replied. "I was there, and I saw how much it took out of you. And I know you. Maybe not for that long, but I know you. And I trust you. That's kind of what I came to tell you last night. Mick — I love him, and I know he's doing this because he and Gav think my judgment's off because of... my dad, and stuff in the past... But he's wrong. And if anyone else takes him seriously, then so are they."

I leaned my head back against the wall. "And what if everyone takes him seriously?"

"They won't. Not all of them. Not even most of them. For

Christ's sake, if you were really liable to use those powers, do they think you'd be working the ticket booth and washing dishes? He said himself, didn't he, that you could make yourself the star? If you were him, you wouldn't have taken this 'shadow' business lying down. To be honest, I think that's probably the one decent piece of advice he could have given you – not that you'd want to use his methods, though."

"Don't remind me. Besides, it's not like I can get his ghost, or whatever it was, to testify on my behalf."

"Then it'll be you and me against the world if need be. But it's not going to come to that, alright? I mean, clearly, you're not working mind control powers against me or I would have gotten up sooner and insisted we talk somewhere else so you don't have to sit on the floor with a sprained ankle. Let's go to the kitchen and get some coffee or something, and we can deal with the rest of them later."

CHAPTER ELEVEN

By the evening, my ankle was recovered enough that I could – slowly – make the walk out to the carnival again, but I found it difficult to make myself useful. I didn't trust my injured foot enough to attempt walking around all night with a tray of snacks or drinks as I saw a few other people doing, and everywhere else I tried to offer my assistance it was declined. With the morning's conversation still running around in my head – *And what if everyone takes him seriously?* – I couldn't help feeling like I was the target of sidelong looks, uneasy stares, and thinly-veiled whispers. Unsure if it was perception or paranoia, I wandered away, needing some breathing room.

I was in no hurry to go back into the heart of the Fairy Glen in the middle of the night, nor did I want to take a chance on hurting myself again, so I settled for finding my way to the small pond by the side of the road. Far enough away from the noise of the carnival, but not too close to the glen itself.

Or so I thought. As I sat watching the clouds drift and break overhead, I began to feel the uncomfortable sensation that I was not quite alone.

This would all be so easy to change. Why do you allow yourself to be pushed to the margin?

"Leave me alone, Sébastien," I replied aloud, already moving to stand up. Clearly, the glen's ability to manifest dead people spread further than I had realized. Or I was losing my grip on reality. Either way, I had no desire to stick around.

I can help you. But the longer you allow them to speak against you, the more difficult it will become.

My eyes searched the darkness, not that it revealed anything or anyone. "Fuck off," I muttered, though I suspected the profanity would amuse rather than offend him. "I don't have time for this. Or you."

For the second time, I found myself walking away from the unsettling voice of my twice-great-grandfather. This time, I let the road take me back to the hostel, deciding that it was the only place I was liable to be left alone.

Sleep was uneasy, and Sébastien's words still rattled around in my head when I woke well before dawn. Careful not to wake Eleanor or Claire – and more than a little relieved not to find anyone sitting on the end of my bunk – I wrapped myself up in a sweater and coat, grabbed an apple from the kitchen and headed out into the dim morning. My ankle felt nearly normal, and my feet seemed to have more sense of purpose than my brain did; I let them carry me past the road to the glen and down through the village instead.

Neither the walk nor the fresh air seemed to be helping much, and I wondered idly how far I was going to have to go to get out of my ancestor's shadow. And then I realized that I had a simple way to find out – in the form of the ferry berthed at the pier. A moment's check on my phone told me that the boat would be departing for the island of Harris within the hour. Harris was connected to Lewis. And Lewis, to me, meant Callanish. The place where all of this had begun. Where better to try and figure it all out?

It was a mad impulse, and yet I bought a ticket, strode on board, and only thought to let anyone know I was going after the ship was beginning to pull away from the pier. *I'm not disappearing*, I texted to Eric, then reconsidered my words. *I mean, I sort of am, but only temporarily.*

I supposed I shouldn't have been surprised by the quick reply. *Need company?*

No, it's okay. Am vacating the general vicinity for today, but I will let you know the moment I'm back.

Okay. Reluctantly, he replied. *If you change your mind or want to tell me why you're taking off, say the word.*

I felt guilty for not telling him what had happened the night before, and more so for not saying just how far I was going – and then there was the fact that I wasn't entirely sure there would be a return ferry any earlier than the next morning – but I knew that there was no good way to explain. It wasn't as if I had a plan, or any real idea what I thought I would accomplish by going haring off to Lewis, but at least it felt like doing *something*.

By the time the boat pulled into the tiny port of Tarbert on Harris, nearly two hours later, I was no clearer on what to do about mindspeaking, or about the spectre of Sébastien. A bus sat near the pier, ready to take me and a handful of other travellers onwards; I settled into a front seat and stared out as we crossed the ragged mountains that separated the two ends of the island. On the other side, the low, waterlogged landscape of Lewis hit me in a visceral sort of way with its familiarity, and finding myself on the streets of Stornoway was frankly surreal. Four months, give or take, since I had been in this place with only a faint hope of finding magicians, and no sense of what that meeting would mean.

Impatient to get to Callanish, I took a taxi rather than look up the bus schedule, and so by barely past lunchtime – not that I had remembered to eat – I found myself standing in the mist outside the visitor centre, summoning the nerve to approach the stone circle. The fact that it was deserted was a relief, at least, but I walked around the perimeter twice before I could bring myself to come within arm's reach of the megaliths; some unwelcome voice in the back of my mind whispered that perhaps there would be no magic in this place after all. Or maybe the stones themselves would turn their backs on me: the mindspeaker who could not be trusted.

A bird's cry in the distance startled me out of my train of thought, and before I could return to it I took a deep breath and laid my palm on the nearest stone. The electric buzz of energy was calmer than it had been in the summer, but still unmistakably present; my eyes welled up at the relief, at the physical connection and the reassurance that something was still open to me. The place was grey and quiet and empty without the tents in the distance, but the magic endured.

And Sébastien had endured, the bastard, for nearly a century before his misdeeds caught up to him. Wasn't I, his innocent descendant, entitled to at least the same? "I'm not giving up magic." It was only saying it aloud, my hand splayed out against the rock, that made me realize that somewhere in the past few days I had considered it. Considered how much easier it would be, in a way, to take that plane ticket home and pick up the threads of my life as if none of this had ever happened. *To hell with that*, I thought, exhaling in relief when no voice answered. Apparently it was the Fairy Glen in particular, and not something common to all magical sites, that let his ghost through. *If I had to travel half a day to a different island to get his voice out of my head, then I'd better make use of it and figure out how I'm going to live with this.*

It was wet, it was cold, and it was a weekday in the off-season; if anyone that afternoon saw or cared that I sat cross-legged for a few hours in the inner circle of stones, occasionally talking to myself, I didn't notice. I had a raincoat and a warm sweater, a phone set to silent and a paradox. If I was to be fully accepted into the troupe of magicians – to get rid of the 'shadow' hanging over me – I would have to convince people that I would not use mindspeaking against them. Or on them at all, or even in their general vicinity. But the only way Sébastien had gained people's trust was *by* using it. And now that his talent was well understood, the mere fact of anyone having faith in me was liable to be taken as evidence that I was influencing their decision. Clearly Mick already believed that to be true of Eric. It almost made me wish that I could summon my ancestor's shade to speak on my behalf – not that he made any kind of character witness.

Darkness fell, and I suspected that I had missed the last bus back to town, but I could get a cab again. Or just spend the night outdoors, at the stones. Maybe I would have some kind of vision, as I had once before, and gain a stroke of insight that way.

It was only the sound of footsteps approaching on the gravel that snapped my attention back to reality at last. My jeans damp through, legs creaking in protest at having sat so long, I staggered to my feet, wondering if I was about to land myself in some sort of trouble. I hoped it wouldn't require me to run. But when two shapes – one tall, one short – came up out of the darkness I realized they were familiar.

"Heather Ross – if I knew your middle name I would use it right now! – what the hell do you think you're doing here?" Eleanor sputtered, stopping a foot away from me, her arms crossed. "You leave a note when you go run an errand in Portree for a couple of hours, but you leave the whole fucking island without so much as a word? Why?"

I didn't know what to say, and I didn't dare look at Eric, so it took me entirely by surprise when he almost suffocated me with a hug. "I think I know why," he said. "And it doesn't mean I'm not pissed off at you right now, but let's at least go somewhere dry and warm. Whatever you came here to do, have you had enough time to do it?"

No great answer had presented itself, but maybe the fact that two people cared enough to follow me all the way to Lewis was a start. "I think so."

It was only then that he released me. "Good. Taxi's waiting, come on. Did you have a plan of where you were going to stay tonight, or were you just going to hang out here and catch your death of cold? Christ, I sound like my mother," he added. When I didn't reply, he shook his head and muttered something under his breath. "El, can you call that backpacker place by the ferry, and tell them we're on our way?"

We walked to the waiting car in silence, apart from Eleanor's brief phone conversation, and the long ride back to Tarbert was quiet as well. But I knew I owed them some explanation, and when we were seated in the common room of what seemed to be an otherwise-empty hostel, I tried to summon one. "I'm sorry you had to come all this way," I began, but my train of thought veered aside. "Wait a second. How did you even know where I would be?"

There was silence for a moment, both of them seemingly trying to will the other to be the one to break it. It was Eleanor who eventually spoke up. "When you said you were vacating the premises, Eric was worried."

"I think I have a right to be," he added. "Given everything. If you had a place over here or something, I probably would have assumed you'd just gone home to regroup. But I didn't really think you'd go all the way back to Canada. Which left a lot of question marks. So I asked El if there was anything she could do to narrow it down."

"You… tracked me?" I asked.

She rolled her eyes. "I wish I was that good, to see you all the way here. But I can do it, to a point – how do you think I get the building blocks for the security map? You must not have been on the boat long, because I could still pick you up, but out on the water. Eric freaked out."

"I did not 'freak out.'"

"You did, a little. Understandable." They were sitting side-by-side on the couch, and she patted his knee before turning her attention back to me. "There are plenty of ways someone could wind up out there, not all of them good. Fortunately, I could see you had a definite trajectory. From there… Well, looking up the ferry schedule was an easy enough way to confirm. And as picturesque as Harris is, it didn't seem likely you were over here out of a sudden burning desire to go touristing about. So…?"

I shook my head. "I don't know; I guess I needed some distance to try and breathe. Without feeling like everything's overshadowed by Sébastien. To try and remember what it was that brought me to all this in the first place. Although part of that wasn't a 'what', it's a 'who'," I added, looking up from the faded carpet to look Eric in the eye. "It wasn't fair of me to just take off like that. I'm sorry."

"Can we please just agree to no more vanishing acts outside of the show? For real this time? I know I've been guilty of it too – no, let me finish," he added, holding up a hand before I could open my mouth. "And if you need some space, I'm not going to stalk you, but maybe just… let me know you're in one piece next time?"

He looked exhausted; they both did. I was starting to shiver in my damp clothes, and had no concept of what hour of the night it was, but clearly all three of us were now missing the evening at the carnival. "I'm sorry," I repeated. "No more disappearing."

My voice cracked on the last word, and at that Eleanor stood up, extending her hands to both of us. "Right. That's sorted, now for god's sake let's just find some bunks upstairs and call it a day before this all starts to get maudlin. Tomorrow's a do-over."

CHAPTER TWELVE

"Did you get what you wanted?"

In the dim grey dawn, the ferry was pulling us back towards Skye, and Eric and I were standing at the rail, our hands wrapped around takeout cups from the boat's cafeteria. I pondered his question. "I still don't totally know what I wanted, but I got something."

"Let's just hope it's not pneumonia," he grumbled, rolling his eyes a little. "And are you okay to go back?"

"Only one way to find out. It just all feels backwards, though. I'm here as a magician but I'm not supposed to perform. I can't try to win the elders over without them thinking I'm using mindspeaking. And I need magic to iron all this out, but the magic's in the glen and I feel like I can't go there now without Sébastien looking over my damn shoulder."

"To hell with him. Just don't go to the glen alone. I'll go with you, if you want."

I leaned in against his shoulder just a little, though I told myself it was because of the wind. "Thanks."

On the surface, the day seemed to pass normally – whatever 'normal' meant for a pack of magicians. Nobody was treating me differently – no better, but at least no worse than before – and Mick had gone back to Edinburgh for a while. By late evening, though, a thought occurred to me.

"Has Mick been talking to everyone, or is it just Eric and Gavin?" I asked, watching the shifting pattern of blue and white dots that mapped the carnival and everyone in it. Ari was out patrolling, and the night had brought no signs of trouble, so Eleanor and I could talk.

She wasn't surprised by the question, and didn't patronize me by pretending not to know what I was talking about. "He wasn't outright campaigning against you, but enough people heard him trying to sell his case to Eric. It's not going to sway anyone who really knows you."

That took care of Eric, Eleanor, and the Kavanaghs, by my estimation. Probably Luke as well, with a rather larger question mark over Gavin; Ari, I suspected, would take Eleanor's judgment at face value. "And the rest?"

"Honestly?" She perched on the edge of the battered old chair they'd either found or conjured up. "If I didn't know you – and knowing what everyone's heard about Sébastien – I'd probably have at least considered the question, eventually. Rutherford came to it sooner, because he's a suspicious bloke."

I nodded. "Gavin said he's overprotective of Eric, because of his thing with Stasia."

"Well." She made a face. "I'm sure that's part of it. That was before my time, and from what I've heard Eric's well shot of her. But Mick's far from unbruised, as far as women are concerned. Ditto Gavin. Any woman who gets near any of the three werewolves would have a rough ride, even if she was a shop girl in Marks & Spencer."

"Werewolves?" For a moment, I almost wondered if I should take her literally; it might not even be the strangest thing I'd encountered. But then I recalled Eric's performance the night Mick had arrived.

"Goes back to when they were the three young blokes on the scene. Prowling, and all." She rolled her eyes. "Self-designated; I suppose it stuck. But back to your problem."

Distracted for a moment, I gave myself a shake. "Honestly, I would even go back to the glen and try to talk to Sébastien again, if I thought it would help. But all he'd do is try to convince me to use it."

"There is an argument for that, you know. Not the way he used it, I mean," she added. "But if you got good enough at it to really control people, but only if you needed to, like with Desrochers... It'd certainly be handy in my line of work, I can tell you. And with a skill like that, you probably should train in it a bit, to be sure you can control it."

"You think I can't?"

"It's not a slight on you. I just know with some talents more so than others – fire's a good example – the people who have a natural gift for it sometimes have trouble with their magic sort of... leaking out, for lack of a better word, when they're angry, or scared, or that sort of thing. My guess is adrenaline. But one way or another, if you're wanting to prove the point that you're not Sébastien, the last thing you need is to do it by accident."

I thought over her words, my mind snagging on the fact that it might have already happened. "Well, that's a hell of a Catch-22. I've got to train in it to prevent accidentally triggering it, but if I train in it, it's just going to confirm people's idea that I do want to use it. And it's the one damn skill that I absolutely can't practice solo."

"Practice on your friends. I'll be a guinea pig if you need it.

Eric certainly would."

I shuddered. "I can't do that. I'll figure something else out."

Like every first Saturday night in a new place, the evening wound up with a ceilidh, after the last visitors had gone. I suspected that I would not be in particular demand on the dance floor, and found a bench at one end where I could at least watch the action. When Ben came to sit down with me, I took the chance to air some of the things that had been on my mind.

"You were only little when Sébastien died, right?"

He nodded. "Listen, I know that Mick's been saying things…"

"It's not that. Or not entirely that," I interrupted. He didn't know about my run-ins in the glen. "But I'm trying to understand him a little better. Sébastien, I mean. Your mum and dad would have known him…?"

"Yeah, and I'm sure they'd be happy to tell you what they know – not at this hour, mind – but I think they mostly steered well clear of him."

As Mick was suggesting people do to me. "They wouldn't have wanted to be taken in by his tricks."

Ben shrugged. "I don't know how much he really used it on his compatriots. Don't forget, that was only one of his skills – he earned plenty of accolades for his performances, without having to get into people's heads. But if you really want to know about him, it'd be best if you could talk to Aurelia."

Aurelia. I had heard that name somewhere before, though it took a moment to place it. She had trained Manon, who had given me my first and only crash-course boot camp in using magic. Several questions battled for dominance: Was she travelling with us? Was she one of the elders? But the one that I actually voiced first was, "Why her?" Even if Molly and Daniel Kavanagh had avoided Sébastien, I could guess that there were others among the elders who would still remember a man dead since the 1930s. Sofia, for one, certainly must have been one of his contemporaries.

"Aurelia and Sébastien were..." But Ben left the sentence hanging, as the sound of raised voices erupted from the tent's entrance. I followed the direction of his gaze and saw Claire just inside, looking pale; her father might not know what was going on, but I could hazard a guess.

Ben crossed the room to her; I missed their initial exchange of words and caught up in time to hear Claire trying to tell him that it was nothing to concern himself with. "Just someone who doesn't belong here, Dad. It's nothing to do with me."

"Well, you're safe in here, any road," he admitted, giving her a hard stare for a moment before accepting defeat and heading over to join his wife at a nearby table.

"Is that who I think it is?" I asked quietly.

She nodded. "I'm going to have to talk to him. I know I am. But not here, for god's sake. Especially not right now."

"Do you need someone else to go with you?"

"No." Claire shook her head. "I told you, I'm not afraid of him, it's not like that. Not at all. I just... I mean, who could have a personal conversation here, even if they were one of us?"

I looked around. "True."

"I'd just text him, and say to meet tomorrow at the pub or something," she continued, "but of course there's never reception here, probably even if El and Ari weren't doing whatever they do to jam it."

"Let me go tell him, then. If you don't want to go back out right now."

Claire narrowed her eyes a little, as if trying to guess my motives. I had to admit, curiosity was certainly one of them, but there was also the fact that the noise outside was attracting an increasing degree of attention. "Alright. Tell him to meet me… hm. Not the pub. Mum and Dad are staying there; that's all I need. He can meet me at the bus stop at the road end here. Tomorrow morning at eleven. Go on, then, before I change my mind."

I edged past the few curious people standing around, and slipped through the double draperies that separated the magicians' ceilidh from the rest of the world. Outside, I found a scene reminiscent of the front door of a nightclub, with Ari cast in the role of the bouncer: magicians were passing by unchallenged, as one man tried to argue his case.

"You haven't been invited, mate. That's as final as it gets."

"Listen, I just need to talk to somebody in there, for two minutes, I told you…"

I stepped around Ari's tall form and got my first good look at the man Claire had nearly left the magicians for. He looked very young: about my height, with close-cropped dark hair and black-rimmed glasses. "Can I have a word?"

Both men looked startled, but I gestured off down the aisle between the tents. "Walk with me for a sec," I told Brendan. When we were out of earshot of the doorway, I passed on Claire's message. "I promise you, this isn't the time or place to make a scene," I added. "If nothing else, her dad's in there." *And here comes her half-brother*, I mentally tagged on, seeing Eric coming out of the tent.

"Do you think she…?"

"I don't know anything," I replied, before Brendan could finish that question. "Except that if you cause her any distress, there are a lot of people who will make you regret it."

83

He nodded, wide-eyed. Whatever he had deduced about who Claire really was, he seemed to realize that he was dealing in something he did not fully grasp. "I'd... I'd never hurt her. I'll be there tomorrow."

Eric came up to me as Brendan walked away into the darkness. "Who would he never hurt?"

It wasn't for me to break Claire's confidence, though it felt strange to keep anything from him. "It's nothing. Don't worry about it."

"Hmm." He didn't press the question, although I was sure he could put two and two together. There were only so many woman of a relevant age, after all, and even fewer who would have asked me to act on their behalf. "He doesn't look like he'd hurt a fly, although looks don't mean much." After waiting a while – perhaps to ensure that Brendan was actually leaving – he changed topic. "Are you planning on going back in?"

I looked back at the tent. "I hadn't really considered that it was optional. Why?"

"Just something I wanted to talk to you about."

"You sure you don't want to wait till four in the morning, when I'm asleep?"

He rolled his eyes. "Are you sure you don't want to jump the next ferry to Lewis? Look, I'd say we could just take a walk, but I don't think either of us wants to head to the glen right now. Can we go sit down in Eleanor's tent for a few minutes?"

It seemed my evening was coming full circle. "Of course; lead on."

"We're here till Friday," Eric began, motioning for me to take the comfortable chair. For himself, he pulled up a stool. There was no one else in the tent; the lights on the monitor screen were reduced to a tight cluster in and around the purple tent, and nearly all blue. The few white dots made sense now that I knew there were a handful of non-magicians among the company. "I'm going to fly back to Buffalo on the Monday morning, so I can be there for my mom's birthday, as well as Christmas. When are you going back to Canada?"

"On the fifteenth. Two weeks tomorrow." I had had to guess when booking my flight. "I guess I might see if I can move it up, then. Who told you the end date?"

"Ben. But that's not really what I pulled you in here to talk about. Mick's coming back up before we're done. And he's going to want an answer from me, about whether or not I'm going to come up to Edinburgh to join the art centre."

With everything else I'd had on my mind, I had rather forgotten about this. "And... what are you going to do?"

He tented his hands, bringing his fingertips to his lips for a moment before speaking. "I want to. I've been batting it around for years, and it makes a lot of sense. The setup's ideal, there's nothing keeping me down south, I love Edinburgh. And Mick's one of my oldest friends."

"But...?"

"He needs to get off your case, for one thing. I'll be honest: I don't have an easy time putting my trust in people. Life experience puts up a lot of walls sometimes. But I trust you. I have since we met. And... my dad wouldn't have..." He looked away for a moment. "He wouldn't have picked you to come and talk to, if I was wrong about that. Mick doesn't know about that part, but if I say I trust you, that should be enough for him."

I felt as if I had just been handed something very delicate. Swallowing the lump in my throat, I found my voice. "Thank you."

There was a long silence, before he resumed. "And... you're still thinking of Scotland, as far as finding yourself a place, right? Don't worry, I'm not suggesting anything ridiculous," he added, his words accelerating a little. "But I... I love being here, and I love most of the people here, but most of them, if we're a few months between performances sometimes, it's not a big deal. But I might not hold it together so well if I didn't have you to talk to now and then." He said it with a grin, but the levity didn't quite reach his eyes. "If you're going to be up here somewhere, that's a point in favour of moving as well."

It took me a little by surprise to realize that I felt the same. I had been casting about, weighing the options of various places to base myself, but the thought of having him in the vicinity was making Edinburgh, or somewhere nearby, feel like the exact place to be. "Likewise. I mean, I won't really know where I can afford to go till I sell my house, but you're a point in favour of Edinburgh as well."

He nodded, the deliberate grin turning into a proper smile. "There you go. Mick'll just have to deal with it. But seriously, he hasn't been around; he's met you for all of about three minutes. He'll see."

I wasn't sure where the certainty had come from — I didn't share it — but it was hard not to be cheered by his show of confidence. "I hope so. Can I... ask you something?"

"Of course."

It was my turn to stumble over words, as I recounted what Eleanor had suggested. "I need a second opinion," I concluded. "I feel like — especially if people are already worried about me abusing it — I should just steer right the hell away from mindspeaking, not even play around with it. But the more I think about it, I'm a bit worried about what she said, that it might manifest itself when I don't mean to."

Whatever question he might have expected, this clearly wasn't it. After a long pause, he pulled his chair a little closer. "El's relatively new here, and I think accidental magic is pretty rare, once people get past finding out that they can do it in the first place. But as far as safety goes, she knows what she's talking about. There's probably some merit in the idea. But who would train you?"

I held out an open hand. "That's the thing. There's really nobody, is there? I mean, Ben mentioned someone named Aurelia, who I guess knew Sébastien, but I'm sure if she'd had the same talent I would have heard about it by now." In my mind, I heard that sentence that had been cut off: *Aurelia and Sébastien were...* Friends? Enemies? Lovers?

Eric shook his head. "I've heard the name, but I don't know who she is. One of the elders, I assume."

"But the other thing Eleanor suggested," I said, wanting to bring things back to the point, "is that I self-teach. Practice on friends. She offered, but also said I should use you as a guinea pig."

That grin again. "Of course. I don't know if I'd be that good a test subject, though."

"I mean, I wouldn't ask you to do that; I thought it was out of line to begin with," I replied hastily.

"No, honestly, I'm happy to help, if you want to test it out. I just..."

"What?"

He looked away for a moment, as if deciding how to answer, then turned back to me. "It just might not be the best test, trying to mindspeak me into doing something. I can't think of much you'd ask for that I wouldn't already want to do." For a few long seconds, it seemed as though those words were hanging in the air between us. "So, you know, it'd be a bit of a challenge," he added, and the tone came back to normal. "Now come on, I'm sure people are forming all sorts of ideas about where we've gone by now." Extending a hand, he helped me to my feet.

"Wait." As soon as I'd said it, I realized I had no idea why I was stalling, and I struggled to come up with some reason. "I've... I've never seen your paintings. Talking about the art centre, I don't know why I never asked before. Do you have any pictures?"

He looked gratified, if a little surprised. "And here I thought you would have found out everything about me by now."

"You know, I thought about it so many times, especially when I went back home after Callanish. I think I was afraid to try and reconcile magic and real life. To be completely honest, I think some small subconscious part of me was afraid you weren't actually real."

"Too good to be true," he joked, giving me a hug. "Pretty sure that's the first time I've been called that."

"You know what I mean."

"Yeah, I do. I remember that feeling. And I did look you up, or tried to. There are a hell of a lot of Heather Rosses out there, you know. But about the paintings... I do have some photos, but will I sound like a total ass if I say I'd rather show them to you in person? I mean, if you change your mind later about searching me, there's a bunch of pictures on my art website, but I feel like photos strip some of the life out of them."

"I guess I'll have to wait and see them in Edinburgh, then," I replied. "But I'm curious now. You'll have to hurry up and move."

Eric laughed. "You too."

CHAPTER THIRTEEN

Sunday morning, I was woken early – by magician standards, at any rate – by the sound of pacing feet. Opening my eyes, I saw that it was Claire, going back and forth from the hallway washroom far more times than necessary, changing clothes three times and putting her hair up, then down, then into a single long braid.

"You'll be fine," I said quietly, making her jump. After pulling on some clothes, I motioned for us to leave the room before we woke up Eleanor.

"I know. It's just not going to be an easy conversation. But he deserves to know why we can't be together."

She was now fidgeting round the kitchen, her nervous energy undimmed. I watched her for a minute or two before replying. "And you're still sure that's true?"

"What do you mean?"

I gestured to her skirt, and her makeup, neither of which was customary for her during the day. "You look a little dressed up for someone who's sure there's no chance."

Claire closed her eyes and took a deep breath. "I know, but... could you not, right now? I don't ask you about my brother."

It was true. "You're right; I'm sorry. I know this has got to be hard enough, without me putting my two cents in. Good luck."

"Thanks." She glanced at the clock: a quarter to eleven. "I'm going to go, before I lose my nerve. We'll just walk and talk, and hope not to run into my mum and dad along the way."

As she headed towards the door, I thought of Ben's concerns the night before, and the fact that he or Colleen might well have occasion to be walking up the road on what looked like a fine Sunday morning. Then I thought of our interrupted conversation. "Don't worry about your parents," I said. "I'll keep them busy."

It took me a couple of minutes to retrieve my coat and bag, so by the time I was walking down the hill, Claire was already waiting alone at the bus stop. Giving what I hoped was an encouraging smile, I left her to it.

As I got closer to the village, where reception was better, I pulled out my phone and sent a quick text asking Ben and Colleen to meet me for a cup of tea. *Just sitting down to late breakfast, come and join us* was the reply.

The pub was a traditional affair: dark wood, heavy beams, slightly threadbare red carpet. "There you are, darling," Ben said, standing up and pulling out my chair. An old-fashioned gesture of politeness – but then, he was closer in age to my grandparents than my parents, despite appearances. "Have you eaten?"

I had not, which meant more small talk while he went to the bar to retrieve me a cup of tea and add a third plate of breakfast to their order. Only when the food had arrived did Ben allude to why I might have turned up at their table. "I'm sorry that commotion broke off our conversation at the ceilidh," he said, stirring a little milk into his tea. "I looked for you afterwards, but someone said you were away with Eric."

As a reflex, I glanced at Colleen, but her attitude towards Eric had thawed a fair bit in recent weeks; she said nothing. "You had mentioned Aurelia," I prompted.

"Ah, yes. If you truly want to know more about Sébastien, she would be the one to talk to."

"She knew him?"

Ben nodded, taking a moment to finish a bite of food. "Better than anyone, save maybe Raffaele — and even if he was still living, he worshipped the man."

"And Aurelia didn't."

"No. The two of them were rivals, you see. Aurelia, at any other time of our history before or since, probably would have been a superstar, unparalleled in her time. But just as her fortunes were rising, in comes this upstart who's just as talented, if not more so."

"Or perhaps, *nearly* as talented," Colleen put in, "but conveniently having the ability to shape people's opinions the way he wanted them to go."

"Touché, love." Ben gestured his acknowledgement. "There's no denying he was a great magician, but the finer points of how great? I guess that's hard to say, with him. He and Aurelia were like two planets orbiting round each other, to hear Mum and Dad tell it, the competition driving them to new heights. They depended on each other, in a way."

I thought this over. If Aurelia had already been practicing her craft when Sébastien arrived on the scene... I couldn't make my brain do the math. "And she's still... Is she here?"

They both nodded. "She rarely sees anyone," Colleen said. "Even less so than Sofia. Her performances now are set pieces. Have you been through the tent with the flowering tree?"

I had, just the night before. It had seemed simple at first: a tent with a bare tree at its centre when I'd walked in. As I'd watched, the branches had begun to give off a soft, elusive musical sound as they budded, then blossomed with small globes of shifting, multicoloured light. By the time the tree was covered, the first of the spheres had begun to float upward; as they reached the silken ceiling, it was impossible to tell whether they vanished or passed through it. Finally, the tree had ended as it had begun: bare, skeletal, and seemingly void of life. The piece had the sort of spooky beauty that drove home to me just what a strange thing it was, to live in a world of real magic.

"Even I haven't seen her in... it has to have been a year or more," Ben added. "She rarely comes to meetings. Though with all the discussion around your newfound talent, and where it came from, I wouldn't be surprised if she lands up taking an interest."

"And if she does?"

"Good question. More tea?" Without waiting for an answer, he refilled my cup from the teapot in the windowsill. "There's no telling how she'll feel about your connection to Sébastien. But I suspect she'll be curious, all the same."

CHAPTER FOURTEEN

Aurelia was clearly not someone who I could just find and ask for information, so I tried to put her out of my mind. I certainly had plenty of other things to think about.

Having made the commitment – at least in principle – to move to Edinburgh, I was suddenly impatient to make it happen, perhaps because it still seemed unreal. There were so many loose ends to tie up, not least of which my family, who were still grappling with my decision to leave for Europe. Christmas would be interesting, to say the least. And there was still plenty to resolve on this side of the Atlantic. Even if I was starting to understand the 'shadow' over me, for the moment I wasn't much closer to working through it.

These thoughts carried me most of the way back up the hill from the pub. Coming to the now-empty bus stop, I decided to sit down, take advantage of the sunshine and quiet, and give my overtaxed brain a rest. Looking out over the ruffled blue of the bay, I reflected that despite all the question marks, there was no longer any doubt in my mind that I was in the right place. Maybe everything that had happened in my life had just been stage direction, to bring me to the magicians.

"Planning a disappearance?"

The voice startled me; I hadn't realized I was so lost in thought. Eric walked up, his boots crunching on some loose gravel at the roadside. "No," I replied, laughing a little. "In fact, just thinking about how there's nowhere else I'd rather be right now." I had meant it broadly, but as I said it I realized that it applied to the exact moment I was in as well.

"Good." He sat down beside me on the bench and nudged my shoulder with his. "Because there's no buses on Sunday."

We sat in pleasant silence for a while, only the occasional far-off bark of a dog or bleat of a sheep carried past on the breeze. Eric was curling and uncurling the fingers of his right hand in an elegant arc; when he noticed me looking, he added a little flourish of blue-tinged mist off his fingertips. It was gone as soon as it appeared, blown away towards the open ocean, and there was not a soul in sight – but still, it seemed a bit of a cheeky thing to do magic so openly at the roadside in broad daylight. I couldn't help a laugh.

"What?"

"It just made me think of when I met you," I replied. "Not the very first time, but when I ran into you in the gallery in Stornoway. You said we'd be seeing more of each other, and that you could help me with what I was looking for. Until I looked at the card you gave me, I had just about written you off as completely cocky and full of yourself."

"And you've just realized you were right?"

"I haven't made up my mind yet," I joked. "But really... the fact that we met in Edinburgh, and then on the ferry and at the gallery: I wonder if I still would have wound up here, if I had just turned up at Callanish without knowing anyone."

He shrugged. "It would have worked out."

"I don't know. Nobody else was exactly falling over themselves to introduce me round and believe I could do magic." I wasn't sure what was taking me down this train of thought, and I wasn't sure I believed in fate, but now that I was pondering the odds it did seem like something had been working in my favour. "And I know I said when I joined, that I didn't want to be your protégé, but if it wasn't for you I might be back in Canada with just memories right now. Thank you."

"You don't have to thank me." Putting an arm around my shoulders for a moment, he gave me a half-hug. "If you hadn't been here when I came back after my dad died, I might've fallen back into some old bad habits – so if we're keeping score, I'd say we're even. I…"

"What?"

A long silence, then he shook his head. "Nothing. Come on, let's go back up and get something to eat; Gav's cooking."

When we returned to the hostel, there was an enticing smell of spices and onions in the air, but precious little actual cooking happening when I poked my head around the door of the kitchen. While a pan sat unattended on the stove, Gavin and Eleanor were several feet away, in the midst of what seemed like a heated conversation. Neither of them took any notice of me.

"I'm just looking out for him," Gavin was saying.

Eleanor waved a hand in dismissal. "Nobody's expecting you to do any less, but seriously? You think he's stupid?"

"No…"

"You think just because his dad died, that he's got no judgment whatsoever?"

"No, I…"

Although she had to look up several inches to stare him in the eye, she clearly had the upper hand. "Then trust him. He trusts her, and so do I."

"It's not that I don't want to trust her. I like her. In other circumstances I'd say she's probably good for him, in fact. But, with what she can do... how can he ever be absolutely sure that his mind's his own when she's around?"

Eleanor actually laughed in his face at that. "How can anyone be absolutely sure their mind's their own, when they're... Bloody hell, Heather!" she added, startling at the sight of me. "Did you just get in?"

I pretended I had heard nothing. "Yeah. What's cooking?"

Gavin made a show of poking about at the pans. "Sausage, and frying up some of the cold mashed potatoes with onions. Do you want some eggs?" Eric caught up to us in the kitchen and engaged him in conversation, so I drifted back out to the common room after Eleanor.

"I suppose you heard a fair bit of that after all, yeah?" she said, in a slightly resigned tone. "Sorry. Didn't mean to be talking out of school."

"I don't know; it sounded like you were on my side there. Anyhow, I'm getting used to it. It's nothing I haven't asked myself."

A phone rang somewhere, and it took a moment of looking around before I realized it was actually a landline, on the kitchen wall; Gavin picked it up and spoke briefly, looking incredulous towards the end. "Er, Heather," he said, coming out to find me. "It seems that Aurelia is on her way up here to talk to you."

Although I had thought that all the elders were staying down in the village proper, it was only a minute or two later that a knock sounded at the door. Glancing around at the others, I went to open it. My first thought was that this could not possibly be the woman I'd heard about: Aurelia was a contemporary of Sébastien's, and the person I saw before me looked as though she could barely be a day over fifty. But then, I was not sure how old I should have expected her to appear, seeing as she had to be closer in age to two centuries than one. Her hair was pulled up into a bun, and she wore a woolen coat and a long tweed skirt.

"Um, you must be Aurelia," I said, a trifle belatedly. "I'm Heather. Please, come in."

"Is there somewhere where we could speak privately?" she asked, with an accent that I could not remotely place.

Wide-eyed, Gavin gestured towards his rooms. "Please. Use my sitting room. Can I... get you ladies some tea?"

If Aurelia noticed our awkwardness, she did not show it. "Thank you."

"So," she began, when we were seated on Gavin's threadbare couch and chair, the door closed behind us. "You would know more about Sébastien. So that you may know more about yourself."

"I... I suppose so. Yes."

She looked me over. "I have been a magician all of my years, and those years have been many, as I think you know. I am, most likely, the oldest one who still comes along with the group on our travels, though of course in polite company one does not ask one's friends their age. And after spending so long among such people, and seeing such changes as I have, I have become very much interested in keeping the history of our troupe. Our people, so to speak. And in these many years, I have seen all manner of talents: some suitable for beauty, some for utility. And some that could be put to nefarious ends." I could feel her gaze upon me, sharpening with each passing sentence, though her voice remained level. "But the way in which Sébastien could control the mind of another – this was something without precedent, and something that was thought to have died with him. Until you."

I wondered where to start. "What was he like?"

"He had power, and he was able to learn to wield it without any guidance from other magicians," she went on. "By the time he came to us, he had already found a way to live in the world, but he craved the attention that performing could bring."

"And when did people realize that he was an amoral jackass?"

"That is an interesting characterization." With an almost-silent laugh, Aurelia looked away for a moment. "It is not wrong, perhaps, but you must remember that it was a different era. Though moral codes were stricter in many ways, in others the world was a more callous place, particularly towards what was once called the 'weaker' sex. If he was a seducer of women, most people – including many magicians, then – would have laid the blame at the feet of the women. If people seemed to do his bidding more often than not: well, he was a persuasive man. He did these things seamlessly, without apparent resort to magic, and it was only much later that he began to boast outright of his other, invisible, set of skills. He came to us not long after I completed my apprenticeship to join the troupe. It was..." She thought briefly. "Eighteen fifty-one, or perhaps fifty-two. I remember the first day he walked among us. We all have our own ways to perceive magic on each other: for me, it is something like a golden light, very subtle. Sébastien was almost blinding. And he recognized me as well."

"And that was why you ended up being rivals?"

She made a vague hand gesture. "That was the term most used. I tended to think that we danced round each other – or perhaps, sometimes, paced in circles like two tigers in a menagerie cage. I was always curious to know how he discovered his magic, but he was a closed book. Almost nothing is known of his life before he came to us, and I am the only one left who remembers his early days. He was well entrenched in the group, even by the time Sofia grew up. I am the only one who saw his decline."

I blinked. "Decline? I always heard that he was one of the best magicians."

"Oh, he was. Indeed, he was. But you misunderstand. His decline into the grasp of the sinister side of his talents. He was already a manipulator, already a narcissist, but using his gifts to get his own way, not only under duress but in everything – it was something that he eventually seemed unwilling, or perhaps unable, to control. Rather like watching someone succumb to the lure of other deadly pleasures, like absinthe or opium."

And indeed, I supposed his behaviour had killed him in the end. His son, Desrochers, had certainly displayed the sort of temperament that would not be out of place in an addict. All the more reason for me to take great care in how I used the mindspeaking – if I used it at all. "I just have one question," I said eventually. "You spent a lot of time around Sébastien, and you knew what he was capable of. Is there any way to block his power? The mindspeaking?" In my experience, I had been able to combat Desrochers, at least somewhat, by using the same skill back against him. But that was not what I meant.

Aurelia narrowed her eyes a little, and looked me up and down. "Do you ask because you want to protect people from yourself?"

"If I can't do that, how can anyone ever trust me?"

A genuine smile. "I can see that you are very unlike him. Yes, I can teach you. Let us begin." Standing up and stepping away from the table, she began to reveal her secrets. It was a simple enough technique on the surface, but Aurelia reminded me that it would take a great deal of practice before it would have much success against a proficient mindspeaker. "This will suffice, for now, to protect your friends should you slip up," she reminded me. "But you will need to make them understand that it is to be taken seriously. A mere hour's instruction would not have equipped anyone to stand up to Sébastien at the height of his powers."

"How did he get so powerful, anyway?" I asked. It was a recurring theme when people spoke of him.

Aurelia looked at me, as if debating how – or whether – to answer. "He was closer to the source."

"The source of what? Of magic?" I asked. When she nodded, I added, "Does anyone actually know what that is?"

"No, we do not. Not for certain. Whether it came about suddenly, or gradually, and if there was only one originator... We do not know." Resting her elbows on the arms of the chair, she tented her fingers. "Our history is lost somewhere in the distant mists of time. But there is this: over all the years that I have known, and all that those before me knew, there were all manner of magical practitioners, some capable of greater things than others. Talent, intelligence, creativity, hard work – all of these things can set a magician above their fellows, just as in any human endeavour. But the fact remains that some magicians have more... magic, than others. Greater potential. Whether or not they make the most of it, that energy that is at the heart of all we do, is present in larger quantities in some among us. Whether it is known from birth or discovered later in life does not seem to make a difference."

"And... that means they're closer to whatever the origin of magic was?" I asked.

Aurelia nodded. "So I believe, in any case. There are tales, rumours, going back generations... It may be that there was one person, or a small group, from whom all of us claim descent. When I was a girl, it was sometimes whispered that the First Ones still walked the earth, possessing so much magic that they are more or less immortal."

Despite everything I had been through in the past months, this still seemed like a step into the unbelievable. "Sébastien can't have been one of those. He's dead, for one thing."

"I do not know of anyone who claims to have seen these First Ones, nor yet know who they might be, if they even exist. And no, I do not claim that Sébastien was one. Nor even close. But in, say, a thousand years, how many generations would you expect?"

I thought for a moment. "About thirty, give or take?"

"Yes. If we were to imagine that the source of magic was a thousand years ago…"

"It could be fewer generations, though, couldn't it?" I interrupted. "If magicians live longer, and can have children later…" As I said it, I realized that I only knew this to be true of the men, but I supposed the effect of magic on the human reproductive system was not necessarily the issue at hand.

She held up a hand. "Well, let us not split hairs. And the origin of our magic almost certainly goes back further than a millennium. But for the sake of example, let us say thirty generations. At least some of those early magicians would have had children by ordinary people. As indeed, some do today. Anyone who is a magician alive today carries only a dilute amount of the original magic, and yet we can do great things. Molly Kavanagh can trace magic in her family back at least to the fifteenth generation in her mother's line, but her father's father was an outsider. So her portion of magical energy is lessened by the many steps removed from the source – even supposing it was the fifteenth generation back, which it assuredly was not – and by the introduction of other bloodlines. She is a tremendously gifted magician," she went on, "but you see that she is aging. Part of this is because she withdraws from magic; many do, as time passes, in deference to what would normally be the span of a human life. But that is not the whole of it. She is further from the source."

By this logic, Aurelia must reckon herself to be closer to this 'source', whatever it might be. "And you're what, twice her age?" I knew the question was impolite. "Are you saying you're better than her?"

"No." She closed her eyes and sighed, with the air of someone who had been asked the question many times before. "This is the reason I rarely speak of these matters. I do not hold it as anything more than a curiosity, perhaps some small explanation for the mysteries of our existence. As I said: talent, dedication, genius, these are all far more important than some accident of the bedchamber. Molly Kavanagh has all of those qualities, and many more things that make her a commendable human being as well as an exceptional magician. But imagine that Molly is perhaps twenty-five generations distant from the first magician. What if Sébastien were only half that?"

From all I knew of him, he had come out of nowhere and had been the 'five hundred year storm', according to Ben's description. If he were closer to some theoretical common magical ancestor – and assuming that Aurelia was correct in the idea that magical power was diluted with exogamy and the passing of time – that might indeed explain his prowess. It left another question, though. "But wouldn't his parents have been magicians, then? At least one of them?"

"Are yours?" Not waiting for an answer, she carried on. "And Sébastien, to my knowledge, was born around eighteen-thirty, somewhere in the Auvergne. His parents would have come from the barest cusp of the nineteenth century, in a rural, Catholic place. If they did possess magic – and if they were even aware of it, as many people are not – who is to say that they would not have viewed it as the work of the devil? Something to be feared and suppressed? Perhaps even beaten out of a child; who knows? He never spoke of his family, so these are only my suppositions. But I am sure you can think of many reasons why a person alone might have shied away from magic in that place and time. Far more surprising, truly, that anyone was bold enough to embrace it without a community to guide them. But to be so gifted as he was, it does not come from nowhere." She paused for a long time. "I hope that you will handle these gifts with more care."

CHAPTER FIFTEEN

Aurelia departed without a word to any of the others, even though quite a crowd had gathered in the common room by the time we had finished. I was left standing in the hall, feeling the weight of everyone's curiosity hanging over my head. Doing my best to ignore the inquisitive looks, I retreated to the relative sanctuary of my dorm.

Eleanor poked her head round the door a few minutes later. "Everything alright?"

"Are you asking, or is he?" I replied, raising an eyebrow.

She laughed. "Well, he didn't say it, but he's hovering out in the yard. If you want to go out the back way here, you can avoid the rest of them, though they'll be mostly over it in a few more minutes. Did you get the answers you wanted?"

"Some of them. The most important one, I guess." Tilting my head, I looked at her. "You know when you said you'd be a guinea pig, if I ever wanted to practice that mindspeaking? You still up for it?"

"Nah, don't think I am, actually." But then she shook her head. "Alright, yes, I am. Just had to test, you know. No offense."

If I was being honest, I was a little taken aback, but at least she was being upfront about it. "No, I get it. It's just... Aurelia's said she knew how to block it, with Sébastien. And if I want to be able to teach people how to do that, I need, well..."

"A lovely assistant," Eleanor finished for me. "Absolutely. If nothing else, it'd be a great opportunity to learn from her, even if it's indirectly. But if she's known this all along... Okay, granted, as far as I know nobody else has had the ability since he died, but why not share that knowledge when he was still around, I wonder?"

I shrugged. "Maybe nobody ever thought to ask."

"And you're not asking Eric to be your test subject, because...?"

There were too many thoughts jostling about in my head for me to dissemble. "Because he told me himself he'd be a terrible specimen, because he couldn't think of anything I'd tell him, that he wouldn't want to do. Happy?" I added, unnecessarily, for the expression on her face was obvious.

"I'm not saying a word," she replied, all the while looking as though she was trying not to laugh.

I told Eric the outline of what I had learned from Aurelia, and that Eleanor and I would be spending some time working on the techniques. He didn't pry further; I knew he had other matters on his mind, as we drew closer to the end of our sojourn on Skye. Among the issues weighing on his shoulders was Mick's impending return – now apparently postponed till our final night – and then of course, the prospect of seeing his family again.

"I don't think they understood why I left so suddenly, when I got the Masquerade invitation," he told me, as we took a walk to the glen in the fog on Thursday morning. I was in no hurry to go back there at night again, but it seemed innocuous enough in the weak light of day. "My mom must know by now, more or less, what it is I do here, but my brother and sister – there's no good way to explain it, without dragging my mom into the midst of things to corroborate it all, and that's the last thing she needs to deal with right now."

"I hope they can get past it without too much drama." I knew that in the aftermath of his father's passing, his younger brother and sister had found out, belatedly, about Eric having been John Heyward's adopted rather than biological son. "Will you have a lot of other relatives to see over Christmas, or is it just you guys and your mom?"

He looked off into the mist. "I don't know what we'll do. You'll still be over there for New Year, right? Maybe I'll come up to Toronto." Then he stopped walking, turned to look at me, and changed the subject yet again. "Say you'll perform tomorrow night."

"What?"

"To hell with what anybody else thinks. You've been working away and helping everyone else out; it's time to do something for yourself, at least once while we're here. Seriously," he added. "You're still so new at this. And you're going to be away probably at least a month, dealing with everything back home, and then there's not a lot going on in the winter. Just perform once… to keep in the habit, if nothing else."

I started walking again, needing to move in order to think about what he'd said. We were into the glen itself by this point, and I chose a path at random, coming around one side of the little pond. The hills loomed out of the fog here and there, and my voice sounded odd when I spoke again. "I don't know."

"You were all set to go, until that meeting with Sofia," he pointed out. "What's really stopping you?"

Before I could think how to reply, another voice spoke. "He

asks a good question. Perhaps you should listen to him, even if you choose not to listen to me."

My eyes went to Eric's face: had he heard it, or was it in my mind? But it was clear the voice was real; his head was swiveling, trying to locate the speaker. "Who's there?"

"It's Sébastien," I answered, raising my voice a little, though I moved closer to Eric's side without really meaning to do so. "Come out, then, if you can. If you want to talk to me. Let's do this face to face."

There was silence. And yet somehow I knew he was still there. To whatever extent he was there at all, that is. "Go on, then, show yourself," I prompted, after several seconds. I had been more than a little frightened by my last encounters with Sébastien's ghost – was that what he was? – but this was different. It was daytime, and I was not alone. And I had spent so much time the past several days mulling over his influence on my life that I was frankly getting fed up with him. "Let's meet properly. In the last little while I've met a great-grandfather who should've been long dead, a grandfather who died early, and the ghost of my best friend's dad." Out of the corner of my eye, I was aware of Eric turning to look at me, maybe because of my choice of words, but I forged on. "Not to mention having a nice catch-up with my great-gran. Your daughter. You called her Christiane." It was a mark of where my life had gone in recent months that it seemed perfectly logical to be standing in a thickening Scottish fog, brazenly baiting a man who'd been murdered nearly a century before. "So why shouldn't I see your face? Anything you've got to say to me, you can say to Eric."

"You trust him implicitly." The voice was no louder, but it seemed more substantial, in some way that I could not put my finger on. "How touching."

At those last two words, a shape formed within the mist,

gradually deepening and taking on form and features. More than anything, it seemed like one of Eric's own performances – so much so that I found myself glancing at him. "This isn't me," he said quietly, taking my hand.

The shadow resolved itself into the form of a man. He stepped forward, looking almost solid, but not quite. Sébastien was not a tall man: shorter than me by a few inches, in fact. If I had not known him to have been my Granny Chrissie's father, nothing would have stood out to declare that fact, but looking hard I could see a slight resemblance, mostly about the eyes and jawline. He certainly looked nothing like me. His pale hair was pushed back from his forehead and his clothing was that of a late-Victorian dandy. If I had been asked to assign an age to him, I might have guessed thirty. Though with him, that meant nothing, of course.

Of course, came the voice inside my mind.

"Oh, no," I said aloud, shaking my head. "Like I said, anything you want to say to me, you'll say to both of us. Out loud." To reinforce my point, I drew in energy and wove it into a wall around my mind, just as Aurelia had taught me. Just as I had been teaching Eleanor. I was beginning to regret not having taught Eric.

Sébastien had started to smile, but his brows furrowed, eyes narrowing slightly. "You have grown stronger, child. My worthless son will certainly pose no further danger to you, should the two of you meet again. No need for the bodyguard," he added, tilting his head in Eric's direction. "But then, you have other uses for him."

A smug expression adorned his hazy features. My mental defenses were still holding, but of course he had already stolen a glance at some of my innermost thoughts during our first encounter in the glen. "I don't use people. That's where we're different."

Sébastien shrugged, in such a way as to suggest not so much acquiescence, as a complete lack of interest in further arguing the point. "Call it what you like. You still haven't answered his question. Why have you not taken your proper place in the spotlight? If this stray bastard can put on a show, then certainly you should."

"He can say what he likes about me," Eric said, his tone betraying nothing. "Don't let him rattle you."

"And here I thought that we were in agreement." Sébastien turned to look Eric in the eye for the first time.

"That Heather should perform? I think if she wants to, she shouldn't let someone else's opinion hold her back," Eric replied, as casually as if he were discussing the weather – although I noticed he avoided meeting my ancestor's gaze directly. "What your motives are, I haven't got a fucking clue."

The ghost – if that was what he was – looked mildly offended. "Motive? I have no motive. If it is sinister of me to want to see my gift carried on in the world, then perhaps I am as evil a villain as they have painted me."

I could see that Eric was about to reply, but I spoke first. "Funnily enough, I believe you. In a way. You want me to perform – or, more importantly, you want me to use magic the way you did – because that's the closest you're going to get now to immortality." It was only in saying it that it occurred to me that it was a relatable impulse: possibly the most human thing in my knowledge and experience of the man. "I forgive you for not understanding. And I suppose I'm glad I was able to speak to you face to face, once," I added, placing just a little emphasis on the last word. "But the thing is, Sébastien – whether I use it or not – it's not your gift. It's mine."

Without waiting to see or hear his response, I turned and walked away.

CHAPTER SIXTEEN

Eric caught up to me before I had gone a dozen strides, but he kept pace with me in silence until we had gotten across the road and a breeze had begun to dissipate the mist.

"Can we… sit down for a minute?" he asked, quite suddenly.

I turned to look at him for the first time since he had spoken to Sébastien. He looked rather pale – and when I stopped to consider it, I had to admit I was a little shaky myself. Despite the damp on the grass, we sat down on the side of one of the miniature hills. "Are you okay?"

He took a deep breath and ran a hand over his face for a moment, then shook himself. "Yeah. That was just… I suppose you have more experience seeing ghosts than I do."

"Not the sort of thing I ever expected to add to my resume." I could still hear the French accent in my brain. "I guess part of me isn't surprised that he showed up in my life somehow, but of all the places… here?"

Eric looked over his shoulder, as if he expected my dead ancestor to have followed us. "The glen does weird things. Legend says that fairies are troublemakers. Instigators. A lot of people have mixed feelings about the place."

I could see why. "I'm glad it happened, though. Especially after talking to him the other times – I had wondered so much, whether it was just something in my own head. I can't tell you how relieved I was when I saw you could hear him as well. And thank you for standing up for me there."

"Always. Though it didn't seem like you needed it."

We sat in silence then, watching the mist thin and disappear, bringing the world back to us. I welcomed all the sensations: the breath of wind, the distant bleating of sheep and rush of a stream somewhere, the dying light in the sky, the solid human warmth of the spot where Eric's shoulder touched mine.

"I don't have a tent."

Though I kept my eyes forward, I could feel the shift in his posture as he turned to look at me. "Are you saying you're going to perform?"

"I'm just saying, I don't have a tent," was all I replied, though I couldn't help a smirk.

"That can be remedied," he said eventually. "But you should also know by now – as long as I've got a tent, you've always got somewhere to perform. Use it yourself, if you want. But if you need an extra pair of hands…"

He held his hands out, palms toward me, in illustration; I turned a little, and rested my right palm against his left. For a moment I just observed how his hand eclipsed mine, before I let our fingers twine together. "I'm not going to say no to that."

There was a long moment where we just looked at each other, before he grinned and pulled me to my feet. "Well, then – what are we waiting for?"

That evening, we just practiced – with a few breaks between, for Eric to go on with his usual performance – and for much of Friday morning we were still at it, but by a little after midday, we had something I was happy with. "Enough for now," I declared.

Eric nodded, though it was clear that the hours of work had taken less out of him than it had from me. "We should get something to eat. Do you want to go down to the pub?" Before I could consider an answer, his phone pinged with a text: one of several that he had been ignoring. I realized who it must be.

"Is that Mick, trying to find you?"

"Probably," he admitted.

I gave him a not-so-gentle push. "Go, then. You have things you need to sort out with him. And I'll probably need you later, in case I start to lose my nerve."

The last part was said jokingly, but he smiled in a way that had nothing to do with laughing at me. "Don't worry. And you're right. Do you want to…"

"Just go," I repeated. I was going to have to get comfortable with Mick sooner or later, but I had no wish to be a third wheel right that minute. "I'll meet you after."

It was past dark when he caught up with me again. "It's official," was the first thing he told me. "Edinburgh, here I go."

"Excellent. Tell me all the other details after." Although we still had hours before we had planned to mount our show, I was anxious to be there, among the tents and lights and carnival atmosphere. "Let's go and visit the Feast while there's still time."

When we got to the field, though, my appetite deserted me. I wasn't sure why my nerves were running so high. After all, I had performed many nights in Belgium, and in Germany. And although the memory of Desrochers was still fresh in my mind, it wasn't that I feared being attacked again. But either way, I found that all I felt like doing was pacing in the tent, running over the steps of the performance in my mind. Though I encouraged Eric to take a break and enjoy the show, he stayed behind, sitting patiently on a bench until I paused for a moment.

"Let's just get it over with," he said. "It doesn't matter what time it is. You'll feel better afterwards, I promise."

And so we began. A quick piece of work to illuminate the exterior of the tent, and create the illusion of a starry sky overhead on the inside, then we waited at the centre of the circle, in a pool of unnatural darkness, as the feet and voices came shuffling in.

My attention was on the series of movements and half-whispered words, precise intention focused upon each one, Eric at my back like a shadow as we slowly turned a circle, conjuring sound and vision. For the audience, it began with a low, undulating noise, not so different from the chanting of monks. Then the false sky came alive with ribbons of light and colour, an improbable series of Northern Lights that shimmered and danced and gave split-second form to figures out of legend.

It was complicated magic for a novice like myself, and the whole working of it lasted not more than six or seven minutes before we were clearing the darkness and taking our bows, my hands trembling with the expended effort. I knew it had come off well, but even so, I was gratified by the applause. Eric cast the final little illusion that let us slip out of the tent unnoticed, and I was glad of it; I barely had the energy left to put one foot in front of the other, let alone summon further magic. Keeping a hand on his arm so as not to lose him in the crowd, I let him lead. It was only when we came into a quiet space that I looked around me and found we'd made it to the tent that functioned as canteen, backstage and break room – and mercifully, it was empty but for the two of us.

"That went well," I sighed, sinking down onto the nearest bench.

"It went perfectly. You were flawless," he replied, leaning in to drop a kiss on the top of my head before sitting down next to me.

"I couldn't have done any of that without you. We make a good team."

He took my hand. "We do."

CHAPTER SEVENTEEN

There was more that I wanted to say – things running around in my head that needed to come out, though I wasn't sure how to articulate them – but at that moment Luke burst in. "There you are. That was brilliant!"

Ben followed a moment later, along with Claire and a pair of women I didn't know, and next thing I knew the tent was full of people coming in for a drink or a break; it was a little overwhelming. There would come a time that it would be a simple thing to mount several shows in a night – or to spend the entire evening in performance, as many of the most experienced in the company did. But for the moment, I found I had to just sit back and let it all ebb and flow around me.

When Eric stood up to accept someone's offer of a beer, his vacated seat was taken by Eleanor. "I didn't realize you were going on so early, so I only caught the last bit," she said. "It was lovely. I just wanted to tell you…"

"What?" I turned to look at her properly. News from Eleanor on the field might not be a good thing.

"Um…" Her eyes darted towards the tent entrance. Following her gaze, my question was answered.

Whether she had chosen the right moment, or, more likely, conjured it directly, no one else seemed to notice as Aurelia walked in and took the seat on my other side. "The echo of my old acquaintance is hanging in the glen," she said. "You spoke with him again?"

"I saw him yesterday afternoon."

She tilted her head, ever so slightly. "He took physical form? How interesting."

After a glance around to confirm that no one else but Eleanor was listening in, I described what had happened. At the conclusion, Aurelia sat back and took a deep breath. "He took the appearance of a time when he was at the height of his powers – when he was just beginning to test how far he could stretch his influence over people. He might have still been redeemable then. But how interesting, that you could bend him to your will, and he could not do the same. You have learned a great deal."

"Thanks to your help. I've still got a long way to go, though."

"As do we all. But it would seem you no longer bear so much of his weight upon your shoulders. In time the others will see it as well."

See it, and trust me. She did not need to finish the sentiment for me to understand the implication. Nor was I optimistic enough to think it would be a speedy process. "I have one or two who understand," I replied. "I can work with that."

She raised one impeccably-groomed hand to my cheek, and studied me for a second or two. "Yes, you can. I will see you again in the spring, Heather Ross."

It was only when she stood to take her leave that the others in the tent began to notice her presence, and a hush followed her like the wake of a ship. By the time she had gone, and the sensation caused by her rare appearance had dissipated, the tent had become so crowded that it was like a scaled-down ceilidh, with voices everywhere and a drink in everyone's hand. I had to look around before I located Eric, off to one side with Gavin and Mick: the three werewolves holding court again.

"Heyward tells me you'll be joining us in Auld Reekie," Mick said by way of greeting as I approached. "Edinburgh."

I wondered if he'd expected me to miss the reference. "Yeah, I am. Once I deal with a few things back home." There was room to sit between him and Eric. "I'm not him, you know," I said as I took the space, my voice low but conversational. "Or any of the other scoundrels in my gene pool. It may take a while before some of you see it, but I'm not him." And then I turned my head away, as if I had not spoken. Mick, for his part, acted as if I had said nothing, though I caught him studying me now and then.

Eventually, the little impromptu party began to break up, as some headed out for performances of their own, or to walk the field, or prepare the actual closing-night ceilidh that would come a little later. "Aren't either of you performing tonight?" Mick asked eventually, after draining the last of his beer.

Gavin said something about going on near the end, after midnight, but Eric just leaned back on the bench and raised an eyebrow. "You were there."

Mick made a vaguely conciliatory gesture. "But I mean *your* show."

Funnily enough, I agreed with him, although I felt some annoyance at his implication that what we'd just done didn't count. "You shouldn't feel like you have to call it quits for the night just because I'm done."

"Fine, then, gang up on me." Eric took a look at his glass, realized it was empty, and stood up to take it back to the trestle table that was serving as a makeshift bar. "I'd better not sit here drinking with the likes of you if you expect me to do a second show in one night." Despite his attempt to sound put-upon, he was laughing. But as he went to leave, he gave me a quick nod of the head that suggested I should go along.

"Mick loves the werewolf thing," he chuckled, shaking his head slightly, when I caught up to him outside. "I'll need to take a walk out to the Glen and recharge a bit before I run through it, but there's something I need to tell you, before I get caught up with that."

"What?"

"Nothing bad," he replied straight away. "I would have mentioned it earlier, but you said no details till after the show. You know I'm flying home Monday…"

I nodded. I'd moved up the date of my own flight back as well, after hearing when the show would end. "I guess you won't be able to stick around and get a lift south with Eleanor, eh? I assume you're flying from London."

"Yeah, and I should take care of a few things there before I go. That's what I wanted to tell you – Mick's heading back tonight, after the ceilidh's done, and I'm going to go down to Edinburgh with him. He wants me to see a couple things at the art centre, then I'll get the train south tomorrow afternoon. Do you want to come with us? You said you're leaving from Glasgow, so maybe it'd work. And you might want to take a look around Edinburgh and get your bearings before you start making plans?"

For half a minute, I considered it. I had assumed he would leave the next day, after the tents were struck, and there was a small stab of resentment that Mick was taking him away early. But the prospect of five or six hours in the back seat of a car with a driver who probably didn't want me there was hardly appealing. "I'd better leave you guys to it. I already told Eleanor I'd go with her on

Sunday, and I think we're going to make an evening of it in Glasgow before I head out. Just... don't disappear, alright? I know you need to go get ready now, but I want to talk to you, before you go."

There was a hint of curiosity in his face at that, but he nodded. "Likewise. I'll see you at the ceilidh."

CHAPTER EIGHTEEN

I would have gone to the glen to collect my thoughts, but I didn't want to get in the way of Eric's preparations. And although I was fairly sure Sébastien would not reappear, I didn't feel like taking the chance. Instead, I opted to walk the fringe of the field, the semi-shadowed areas where only a few tents could be found. As my footsteps took me along the far side, I noticed something out of the corner of my eye, so well camouflaged that I could easily have missed it: a small tent, black symbols on black against the night. I was certain it had not been there on any of the other nights of our stay. Ducking down under the low entrance, I went in.

As I had suspected, I found Sofia, looking every part the oracle that she was rumoured to be. "Heather Ross," she said, inclining her head slightly, and motioning me to sit on the cushion opposite her. "Let us see how you have progressed."

I did not need to be told to hold out my hands to her. Various images sprang up when she ran her finger across the lines on my palm, though the only one that hung in the air long enough for me to study was of a bare branch growing and putting out new leaves. What that might have meant to her, she did not say. As she had before, she concluded by taking my face in her hands and staring into my eyes.

"You are beginning to emerge," she said at last, "from the shadows that were eclipsing you. It is not yet complete, but you have come far. You have resolved many of the questions that clouded your mind, and begun to walk further down the path. But you know all of this, do you not?"

"Yes."

"You performed tonight, though it was the judgment of the elders that you should not."

There was no obvious reproach in her tone, but still, I took a moment to consider my response. "Things have changed since you made that judgment. I felt it was time to take the risk."

Sofia nodded. "And another risk lies ahead of you, of a different sort."

I looked down at my hands, wondering what part of them revealed that. There were any number of risks in my immediate future. But I knew which one she meant, without any need for elaboration. "Yes. I can't leave it alone any longer."

"Ask the difficult questions. It is the best way to step into the light."

When I emerged from the oracle's tent, I could already see the cycling emerald light far down the aisle. I nearly missed the beginning to Eric's performance, and had to content myself with standing in the back as all the benches were filled. The images were as breathtaking as ever, the reaction of the crowd as thunderous, and when he took his bows at the end, I was reminded of the first time I had seen him do this, the shock of the confirmation that he was a magician, even when all other evidence had already suggested it to be true. I wondered if this evening would end in a similar way.

He was gone when I emerged, of course, but the magicians' ceilidh would be beginning soon; I knew I would find him there. I went on ahead to the big purple tent to help prepare, while the last few performances were winding down in the marquees around us. The tables and benches were already set up around the perimeter of the space, but Luke's parents accepted my offer of assistance with the magical working required to multiply a modest quantity of food and drink into enough for several dozen magicians and a few invited guests.

"The loaves and the fishes," Arthur joked. "Sarah always says I'll be getting ideas above my station when I help out here."

"Get on with you," his wife laughed. "Mind you make sure there's enough mulled wine; not all of us are beer drinkers, you know."

A few people wandered in with musical instruments and began tuning up in an unhurried fashion. It was only when one of them struck up a few bars of 'Deck the Halls' that it hit me that we were already a week into December, and that this was the troupe's last night of magical performances for the year. I had been so busy chasing down shadows that I had barely given a moment's consideration to the impending holidays; I suddenly wished that I had thought to buy presents.

The tent began to fill up soon enough, the loose group of musicians playing traditional tunes and the floor crowded with dancers. I saw a wide-eyed Brendan staring about him, a drink forgotten in one hand, his other arm around Claire's waist; I wondered if I had looked that stunned on my first encounter with a scene like this one.

Eventually, I spied Eric – with Gavin and Mick, of course – over by the table of food. His back was turned, one hand gesturing as he spoke, and I didn't think he would see me coming up behind him, but he turned just before I came within arm's reach. "There you are," he said, before briefly finishing off what seemed to be an anecdote about some sort of dinner gone wrong. Leaving the others laughing at the story, he cocked his head and looked at me.

"Do you want to go for a walk?"

We emerged into a clear, chill night, a crescent moon hanging past the midpoint of the sky. Once we were out of earshot of the music and voices, I tried to embark on what I wanted to say. "I need you to do something for me."

"Of course. Name it."

"It's… complicated. You know when we saw Sébastien, and I was able to block him from influencing my mind… It was the technique Aurelia taught me, the one I've been working on with Eleanor. It's simple, but needs a bit of practice to get it right. It was hard to keep him out." The words were spilling out, and I knew I sounded a little frantic, but my nerves were getting the better of me. Trying to keep it as simple and articulate as I could, I explained the details. "Does that make sense? I need you to learn it."

"Do you think I'm going to run into Sébastien again, or is this in case Desrochers comes back?" he asked, his brow furrowed. Clearly, whatever he'd thought I'd wanted to talk about, this hadn't been it.

I shook my head. "No. Although I suppose it'd be handy. But no. It's because of me." His puzzled look made me speed up my words again. "I know you trust me. And I know other people don't. And I don't think that I'd ever use the power by accident, but I need you to be able to block it out. To prove I'm trustworthy. And… we spend a lot of time together… we… probably even more so, if we're going to be living in the same city, and…" It had all seemed so much simpler to say in my head. I couldn't quite look him in the eye, though we'd stopped walking and were facing each other. "And I know, when I was talking to Sébastien, I said you were my best friend – and it's true, you are – but I don't know, I don't want to put a label on things that are maybe just happening naturally, but I don't know if… if that's a totally adequate description, any more, for what we are, or…"

"Heather?"

I looked up, nervously. "Yeah?"

"I have something I need to say, too, and I'm just going to jump in right now because I think it might make things a little simpler. I'm in love with you. I've known it for a while. There's been a bunch of times where I've almost told you, including that night I showed up in your room… but I didn't want to wreck our friendship, or make things weird. And I'm not saying it now to push an agenda, or anything like that. I'm not looking for things to change any faster than they have been. I just needed to say it. Even if you don't feel the same way, I needed you to know. But I think…?"

And there went another shadow, slipping away. I had barely even allowed myself to wonder about it until the last few days, and suddenly it seemed so obvious. "Yeah. I do." Putting my arms around him, I let my head rest on his shoulder. "I still need you to learn that mind-blocking technique, though. Even more so."

"Like I told you once before – I can't think of anything you'd ask me for, that I wouldn't want to do. Including learn a new bit of magic. If it's really important to you, of course I'll do it."

I stepped back to look him in the eye. "It is. I'm really serious about this. Promise me you'll do it."

"I promise." Then he raised an eyebrow. "Now, how do I know you didn't mind-control me to agree to that…? No, I'm kidding… I'm kidding," he added. "But seriously, I promise. And there's nothing flashy about it, so I can easily work on it while I'm visiting my family."

"Okay." The mention of family just made me think of how long it was likely to be before I saw him again, although I wanted to push that out of my mind for as long as possible. Then another thought struck me. "You know, everybody's going to say 'I told you so'. They're never going to let us hear the end of it."

Eric shook his head, laughing. "Let them keep guessing for a while. I don't think either of us wants to rush in and change everything, anyhow. Let's just keep being who we are, and… pick up this thread when we see each other next. And they can put whatever name on it they want."

"You're right. And I suppose we do have a ceilidh to get back to, before they send a search party," I sighed, breathing in the scent of him: dark and faintly sweet, overlaid with the leather of his jacket and the peat smoke in the air. "And we're in no hurry."

"True. So let's go back in, and keep them guessing."

Eric and I said our goodbyes at the end of the ceilidh, before he loaded his things into Mick's car to head south. First thing the next morning, the rest of us struck the tents and packed up the show. By midday it was just Eleanor and me packing our bags into her big white van.

"Did the Kavanaghs give you the first few locations, for the New Year?" she asked.

I nodded, pulling out the magician's cards Ben had passed to me before they'd departed. "Val Camonica – that's in Italy, I guess? Avignon, Mont Saint Michel…" My brow furrowed as I realized there was a fourth card in my pocket. I knew for a fact that Ben had only given me three.

When Eleanor's back was turned, I took a closer look at the fourth card. In a neat, familiar hand, it read: *Toronto, New Year's*. It seemed that magic would shadow me everywhere.

ABOUT THE AUTHOR

Lori Zuppinger is a historian by day, writer by night. She lives in Toronto with her husband, son, and many-toed cat. Her non-writing free time is often spent on books, boardgames and rock & roll (not necessarily in that order). In 2019 she's planning to drive less, walk more, brush up on her lapsed Scots Gaelic, and finally publish that steampunk adventure story – so if you happen to be reading this in some later year, feel free to ask her how that went.

Lori can be found at:
www.lorizuppinger.com
@ratherawkward (Twitter)
@escapistwriter (Instagram)
@lorizuppinger.author (Facebook)

Books in the Magicians' Card series:

The Magicians' Card
The Magician's Walk
The Magician's Shadow
The Magicians Divided (release date TBA)

Other upcoming books by Lori Zuppinger:

Velocitor (late 2019)
The Transmuted (2020)

51459350R00081

Made in the USA
Columbia, SC
21 February 2019